DEBBIE CASSIDY

MW00984592

SHADES OF MIDNIGHT

CHRONICLES OF MIDNIGHT

Debbie Cassidy

Cover by JMN Art

"Harker, wake up!" Ryker's voice was saturated with urgency.

I shrugged off the arms of sleep and rolled onto my back, wiping drool from my chin. "Waaa?"

"Suit up, babe. We got a Code Shade."

I was instantly awake and alert. "Where?"

"Black Wing Mansion is under attack."

My body was already in motion—out of the bed and scrambling for the clothes I'd discarded on the floor. "Time?"

"Three in the morning."

Tidiness hadn't been on my mind when I'd crawled into bed less than two hours ago, and now my trousers were missing. Shit. "Where are the others?"

"We're meeting at the van." Ryker threw my slacks at me.

"Thanks." I pulled them on under my sleep-T and then gripped the edges of my shirt, ready to peel it off, but stopped just in time.

Ryker averted his gaze. "I'll meet you

downstairs."

The door shut behind him, and I scrambled to finish dressing. This was the fourth Code Shade this week—a term coined by yours truly. The last three had been sightings by our operatives trained in spotting the signs. The Deep had been hit first, and several nephs and humans had been infected. After that, two residential areas had been targeted, but I'd managed to expel the shades rooted inside the five humans who were showing symptoms of disorientation and aggression. I'd killed the shades in the humans whose souls had been completely devoured. We'd learned to distinguish between the two. Fully taken humans developed crimson irises, nephs didn't. For some reason, the shades couldn't mask this aspect in a human host like they could in a neph body. So, red eyes equaled no human soul in residence. Killing a shade in a human host that still had his soul was not an option. In burning the shade up, I also burned through the soul. I swallowed, recalling the time I'd killed a shade in a human host whose eyes hadn't turned yet—his screams had echoed alongside the shade's as I'd burned him to a cinder. Now, the shades tended to scatter when I showed up, afraid I'd burn them out of existence, or expel them, but there was only one of me and hundreds of them. I couldn't keep this up forever, especially when they chose to hit two spots at the same time. Fuckers knew I couldn't be everywhere and neither could our officers.

Asher hadn't made a grab for me yet though, which was worrying. I'd killed two of his shades in the Order lair and many since, and yet, he'd stayed under the radar. I guess having the Order's wards all over the MPD building and grounds helped keep the big bad at bay, but still, I kinda just wanted to get it over with—for him to come for me and for me to kick his arse and be done with it. He was a shade just like the rest. So it stood to reason I should be able to kill him, right? It was probably why he was playing coy and sending his minions at me instead. Probably trying to tire me out, and sod, it was working, just not in the way he was probably hoping. Deciding to keep the shade presence in Midnight quiet, deciding to deal with it ourselves, was proving harder and harder with each attack.

My body was wrecked, out of balance, and simmering with power I wasn't sure how to control. It was growing faster than I could use it, expanding within me, leaving my skin itchy and tight. Expelling the shades didn't count, because for that I utilized my aether ability. The only thing that seemed to ease the discomfort was killing them. I hadn't even needed to feed for the past two weeks.

It's all right, we'll figure it out, my daimon reassured. Just like we'd figured out how her darkness had shrouded the light within me, and how my feeding had given her the power to keep my true nature hidden until the time was right. Now it was activated, there was no stopping it.

The others were bound to notice how it was affecting me soon. It was getting harder to hide the discomfort between exterminations. My body was a pressure cooker needing to blow off steam. Thank goodness the fuckers were attacking—I'd get to release some of the excess power. We were coping for now, my daimon and I. No point officially stressing until we had to. Right now, we had a Code Shade, and if they were hitting the Black Wings, then we'd be dealing with soulless hosts controlled by shades—the perfect chance for me to relieve some of the tension.

Zipping up my boots and grabbing my jacket, I headed out the door.

Marika and a couple of the Order of Merlin members met me in the foyer. Ryker was in the doorway, letting the cool night drift in and ruffle my hair. Marika's face was pale, and the dark smudges under her eyes spoke of lack of sleep.

"Sit this one out." I cupped her shoulder. "You may have access to the arcane, but your body is human."

Her lips tightened. "If Ava and her unit can help, then so can we."

More Order members jogged into the foyer. This was their home for now, and thank God we had the space for them. They'd moved in after the shit had hit the fan a couple of weeks ago, and then Ava and her unit had moved in last week. The mansion was quickly becoming operations central, but it wasn't enough. We needed more boots on the ground. More help.

I sighed. "Fine, but then you need to get some sleep. Promise?"

She nodded, and gave me a half-smile. "Okay, Mom."

We poured out of the mansion.

I'd never get completely used to the sensation of flying, especially when my defiance of gravity was dependent on another. Bane's arms were solid bands of steel around me. We were almost at the cliff house. I just hoped we got there in time. The van far below carried Orin, Cassie, River, and Ryker. Another three vans followed, filled with the rest of our officers, the Order members, Ava, and several of her unit.

If the shades were attacking the Black Wings, it meant they were confident in their numbers. It meant we were running out of time.

I was no fan of the winged, but better the devil you know, right? The shades were aggressive and single-minded, and who knew what their real agenda was. Asher had said that they had no grievance against humanity, that their issue was with God and the winged, but what was stopping them from turning on us once the winged were gone? What was their end game, anyway? It was unlikely they'd just sit back and chill out once their objective was achieved. Right now, the winged were the only thing standing between humanity and the shades.

"Your thinking is giving me a headache," Bane said. His breath ruffled the hair at the nape of my neck.

We were flying with his chest to my back. I liked to get an aerial view. "I just hope we're in time to help."

His lips teased my earlobe. "The Black Wings are expert fighters. They won't go down easily."

I suppressed a shiver. "And the shades predate them. Who knows what they can do. They wouldn't be attacking if they couldn't hurt or even kill the Black Wings."

Bane was silent, which told me he had come to the same conclusion.

A horrific thought occurred to me. "You don't think the shades can infect the winged, do you?"

"If they could do that, then why attack to kill them? They would have just taken the Black Wings as hosts. The message that came to me was clear. The shades were attacking to kill, and a dead host is a useless host."

Thank goodness he'd taken it upon himself to fill the rest of the MPD in about his relationship with the Black Wings, otherwise explaining how he'd known they were in trouble would have been awkward.

The screech of tires drifted up to us. We were losing altitude in preparation for landing.

"The others are in," Bane said. "It looks like the shades took down the gates. I'm going to drop you just inside. I need to get to the tower."

"The tower?"

"Abbadon needs me."

He was communicating with Abbadon again.

"Is he okay?"

"I don't know."

Below us, the ground was a sea of bodies in combat, Black Wings against humans and nephs, fifty against at least a hundred. Asher wasn't fucking around this time. He meant to take the Black Wings out of the picture tonight.

Time to kiss the ground. "Okay, do it. I'm ready."

Bane dropped me from a twenty-foot height. I hit the ground in a crouch and was up and running into the fray a split second later. Ryker's scent hit me from the left, and Rivers's from the right.

We surged toward the battle where Black Wings fought shades snug in neph and human skin: a young woman here, a teenager there, an old man, a young girl. It was disconcerting, and my feet faltered. The Black Wings must have been feeling the same distress because they were fighting, but not as hard as they probably could. They held back against the human hosts, their pledge to protect humans forcing them to pull their punches.

I switched to aether-sight, and the human skins melted away, leaving only the powerful long-limbed shades, inky black, crimson-eyed, and lethal. A Black Wing, right ahead of me, jumped back to avoid the swipe of a teenage girl's blade. He ducked and evaded while she slashed with the power of the shade she now was. There was no longer a human soul in that body, and the Black Wing needed to accept that and bloody fight back properly. There was nothing to save here, but he didn't know that. He couldn't see what I could.

The girl laughed. It was a tinkling sound that cut through the grunts and clanks of battle. She made what would have been a lethal strike, but I was already in motion, sliding between her and her target. Her eyes widened at the sight of me, the thing inside her recognizing me for what I was. I slammed my hand onto her face and blasted her with the divine power inside me. Yeah, my daimon and I had made that connection a week ago. Malphas had told me that the weapons had been made from a drop of God's grace, and if the power from the weapons was inside me, then …

The shade screamed as it died, and the body of the girl dropped.

I rounded on the Black Wing. "There are *no* humans here. Just shades. Did you see her eyes? Crimson. The human soul is gone. You get that?"

His jaw tightened, and his eyes blazed with defiance, and for a moment I thought he'd strike me down, but then his wings unfurled, and he raised his head and bellowed, "Strike hard, strike true, there are no human souls here!"

It was as if his words had unlocked the phantom shackles holding the Black Wings back. Shrieks and battle cries rose up like angry smoke. The shades fell under sword and whip and blade, and I set to work, burning them to death with my power one by one while they were incapacitated. They couldn't die from their wounds, but what the Black Wings were doing was forcing them to consider retreat, and in the meantime, I was finishing them off.

I caught a glimpse of Malphas, his face etched in steely determination as he parried against what had once been a Lupin. Shit. Lupins were higher-level nephs, and this was the first one I'd seen infected by a shade.

Ryker appeared at my back, ready to swing his axe to ward off an attack by shades while I incinerated their brethren. Cassie and Orin worked together like a well-oiled machine in the periphery of my vision, and Rivers was to my far left, working back-to-back with a Black Wing while surrounded by shades inhabiting minor nephs. There was no hesitation on his part. Good.

My body burned with power as I took out enemy after enemy. Ryker swung his axe in an arc to force back a wave of shades. Black Wings surged forward to help but ended up cutting us off from each other.

I took out an old guy and then spun to counter the attack of another shade, but he skidded to a halt a meter away. I caught the flash of terror in his eyes as his attention went from the old guy's body and back up to me. He turned and ran. Nope. Not getting away. I broke into a sprint after him, leaped, and tackled him to the ground. My hand closed on the nape of his neck and then he was gone, ash and cinder and death. The human shell relaxed beneath me. But there was no time to breathe because there was a shitload more of the fuckers to kill.

Something landed on my back, taking me down, flattening me against the limp human body. Bones dug into my abdomen and chest, forcing the breath from my lungs.

"Shade killer. Now you die," the voice rasped in my ear.

A blade bit my skin, bringing tears to my eyes. My daimon roared in rage, and then a shadow was hurtling over my head, slamming into my attacker and taking him down. I scrambled up to see the shade that had attacked me pinned under Drayton. My heart slammed into my rib cage, hand coming up to stem the blood flow from the snick at my throat. He'd saved me ... Drayton was still in there. I'd been right!

"Alive!" Drayton slammed the shade's head

against the ground. "Asher wants her alive, you moron."

"I'm sorry, Xavier. I lost my head," the shade said.

The bubble in my chest deflated. He wasn't saving me. Well he was, but not for the reasons I'd hoped.

Drayton climbed off the shade and stood to face me. He cracked his neck and smiled. And then he rushed me. It was unexpected, and my body froze for a fraction of a second too long. His hands wrapped around my waist, and then I was airborne for a moment before slamming back down onto his shoulder, too winded to do anything but dangle like a sack of potatoes.

Fucking hell. He had me.

I twisted and bucked, but he was strong, too strong, and moving *way* too fast. Shit. Wait. This was my chance. I could expel the shade. Get it out of Drayton. I pressed my hand to his back and slipped into the aether. The skin beneath me morphed into the black sinewy body of a shade, larger than the average, with power thrumming beneath its inky skin. This was … different. I delved, searching for a grip, but my ethereal hands slipped and slid against his essence.

His laughter echoed in my ears. "That won't work on me, shade killer. I'm a little too high up the food chain for you to expel. If you want me gone, you're going to have to kill me, and that would mean killing *him* too."

My pulse skipped and jumped. No. Drayton was gone. Xavier was lying now to save himself. I delved deeper, and brushed against something small and bright and pulsing weakly.

Shit. My eyes pricked. Drayton. Oh, God.

The building rushed toward us. Xavier was taking me into the manor. Ryker? Where the fuck was he? Orin, Cassie, Rivers, anyone? But then we were inside the building, climbing stairs. What the fuck?

"Where are you taking me?"

"To Asher."

Shit!

Xavier carried me up the winding staircase to the top of the tower. Even though his body had been invaded, he smelled the same as Drayton, and that damn aroma told my body to relax, that it would be okay, even though my savvy brain knew different.

I twisted one last time, trying to break free and failing. "You don't have to do this."

"Oh, but I want to," he replied simply.

What was I doing trying to reason with Asher's general? But it wasn't Xavier I was speaking to, not really. A part of me was hoping to tap into Drayton—that light inside that was struggling to hold on.

Oh, God. How much longer did he have left before Xavier took over completely? How had he survived this long? A chill ran up my spine. What if this was the way with all neph hosts? Cassie had held on for weeks, right? Why hadn't I thought of that? What if neph souls took longer to die, which would mean I'd killed a ton of innocent nephs tonight believing their souls had been devoured.

Xavier pushed through a door and entered the tower room. Cold air smacked against my ass, seeping into the fabric of my trousers.

"Xavier, you brought me a gift." The voice was mellow, chilled with an edge of dark humor.

I'd only heard it once, but I'd recognize it anywhere. Asher.

"Fuck, no." This voice was rough and bone-tinglingly deep.

Bane.

Asher laughed. "Well. We have what we came for, so we'll be on our way."

I twisted against fake Drayton's back, trying to get a view of the damn room. The bits I could see were unfurnished and had arched, glassless, shutter-bordered windows. And shit, was that Abbadon crumpled on the ground?

"Let her go," Bane demanded.

His voice came from behind me, to my left and out of view.

"Harker? Harker, talk to me," Bane demanded.

"I'm okay." I lifted a hand in a wave.

Xavier slapped my arse. Hard.

I let out a yelp of pain. That fucker was gonna pay for that.

"She took out too many," Xavier said. "We need to end this."

"And we will," Asher said. "Just as soon as I get what is mine. Set her down."

Xavier dropped me. I landed on my side, hip scraping against bare floorboards. The bastard just smiled thinly, and it was easy to see him behind Drayton's chocolate-brown eyes—soulless steel where there had once been warmth. And then I got a look at Bane. He was pinned to the wall by an invisible force, his shirt was torn, his head was bleeding, and his eyes blazed with murderous, impotent intent.

Asher was doing this. Using his host body's magic to hold Bane captive. Had he used it to knock Abbadon out too? He pinned his gaze on me now, scanning and searching for the precious last piece of Merlin's soul.

Satisfaction was a burning ember in my chest. It was my turn to smile, smug as shit. "Looking for something?"

Asher's dark brows slammed down over his obsidian eyes. "What have you done? Where is it?"

I shrugged. "Gone."

"No. That's impossible. If it was gone, then I'd be in control. I'd be free." He turned his hands over as if expecting them to yield the answer to his quandary.

I pulled myself to my feet and brushed the dirt off my clothes, focusing on masking the tremble in my hands. This was Merlin, *the* Merlin, with a tankload of power at his disposal and a shade commander in the driver's seat. He could probably break my neck with a thought, and the only reason I was still alive was because he needed something from me. Something even I didn't know the location of, but at least I knew Ambrosius must still be out there somewhere, existing. I needed to play this right.

"What can I tell you? Ambrosius has a mind of his own. We aren't always joined at the hip." Let him think I still had access to Ambrosius and knew where he was. Let him believe I had the power to summon him.

Asher's eyes narrowed. "But you can call him to you? You can speak to him."

"If I wanted to." Why did I expect alarm bells to go off at my lie?

He took a measured step toward me, his gaze speculative. "Can you bring him here or not?"

My pulse accelerated. If he found out I'd lost my connection with Ambrosius completely, then I was dead. But light bulbs were going off in my head. A plan formed. It was a shitty, weak plan, but even a shitty, weak plan was better than no plan at all.

I lifted my chin. "I can. But I'm *not* going to."

Xavier growled in exasperation. "Commander, she's bluffing. How do we know that when cutting the connection between the host body and the soul, she didn't cut her own connection to it?"

Bastard. He needed to keep his stinking mouth shut. My thoughts didn't play on my face, though. At least I hoped they didn't. Right now, I needed that poker face real bad.

I lifted my chin and smiled. "You don't know. You can't be sure of anything. So, you're just going to have to take my word for it. If you want Ambrosius, then let Bane and Abbadon go."

Asher arched a brow. "You're trying to negotiate with me?" He sounded genuinely surprised. And then the surprise morphed into anger. "You're trying to negotiate with me?" His voice went up an octave.

"Are you deaf or just stupid?"

In the beat of a breath, he was in my personal space. His hand wrapped around my throat, his perfect face contorted in rage. Yes. This was what I needed. Him, up close and personal, so that I could—

"Commander, no!" Xavier cried out.

But he was too late. I blasted him with power, channeling it into him, and waited for the burn, the cinders, and the screams.

And waited.

His eyes widened, and his mouth twisted in a wince—the only sign that I'd affected him. And then the hand tightened around my throat. "Sorry to disappoint, Miss Harker, but you'll need a lot more juice than that to hurt me."

My gut clenched. Plan A had failed. The fucker was too powerful while infused with arcane power. Merlin's power. But plan B was working, because in this moment, his focus was completely on me. And if there was one thing I'd learned about arcane magic since hanging with Marika, it was that it required focus.

Asher had just lost his.

Bane snapped free with an inhuman roar, smashing into me and ripping me out of Asher's surprised grasp. He sprinted for the nearest arch.

"Wait! Abbadon!"

His arms flexed around me, but we didn't stop. We flew straight toward the window and out into the night.

So many dead Black Wings, humans, and nephs. In the humans' case, they'd died a while back, when the shade took them over completely, but the nephs may have been alive and trapped inside their bodies. I'd unwittingly killed them. I needed to tell the others what I'd done. The bodies lay like broken dolls strewn across the clifftop grounds. Malphas, Abigor, and the remaining Black Wings stood dazed and lost amidst the carnage. They'd prepared for battle against their White Wing brothers—a battle that would have taken place in an orderly heavenly fashion. This … this had been anything but.

Ryker slung an arm around my shoulder and pulled me into a hug. "Fucking hell, we thought we lost you."

"We almost did," Bane said. "If not for Harker's quick thinking." He frowned. "That *was* your plan, right? To goad him into attacking you and take his focus off me?"

I sighed. "Yes, Bane. That was the plan." But we'd left Abbadon behind. "The plan wasn't a complete success, though, was it?"

He shook his head and tucked in his chin. "If we'd stopped for Abbadon, then we'd have lost our advantage. Asher's magic at close range is powerful, but it's limited over distance. He confessed as much in a mini-rant. I do believe the shade commander is unhinged. If he ever got his hands on Ambrosius then he'd be unstoppable."

I glanced up at the tower to the east, where we'd left Abbadon. He was gone now. Asher had taken him. "What will they do with him?"

Bane's expression tightened. "I don't know. And dwelling won't help."

I closed my eyes and tucked in my chin. Asher had the Black Wing leader, and there was nothing we could do about it. He'd try and use him as a bargaining chip, no doubt, while continuing to build his army. Killing them wasn't getting us anywhere fast enough. We needed to attack the root of the problem. Cut them off at the knees. An idea bloomed in my mind. They needed hosts to influence our world. So, we needed to take away their supply. It was so stunningly simple it was shocking that we hadn't been focusing on it all along.

"We have to stop the shades from taking hosts." I locked gazes with Bane. "We stop them from replenishing their numbers. It's the only way to fight them. We need to cut off their host supply."

"Great plan," Cassie said sarcastically. "And how do you intend to execute it?"

She was wound tight. We all were, so I'd let her tone slide this one time. "I don't know. But I say we gather everyone: Lupin, Sanguinata, the MED, and Tristan. We tell them the truth, and we get everyone in on solving the problem."

"Finally." Ava threw up her hands.

I arched a brow in response to her outburst.

She grinned sheepishly. "It's the right thing to do."

When we'd thought we could nip this in the bud without causing panic, then it had been fine to keep it quiet. But it'd been almost two weeks, and now this attack … "We can't fight the shades alone. We need more soldiers, and we need more brains."

There was no argument, only a murmur of consent.

Abigor joined us.

I took in his disheveled state, the downturn of his pretty mouth, and the sorrow in his eyes. He'd kidnapped me and held me hostage not too long ago, but it was impossible to hate him right now. Now that he'd lost so many of his comrades, and his friend and commander, Abbadon, had been taken.

I met his gaze and inclined my head in greeting. "We need to formulate a plan to get Abbadon back."

He took a deep, shuddering breath. "No."

Had I heard right? "No?"

His smile was tired and laced with sorrow. "We agreed that if one of us was taken we would assume they were dead. We would not negotiate for their life, and we would take no unnecessary risk to liberate them."

Logic agreed that this was the right move. We couldn't risk a ton of lives to save one. The threat to our world was too great, and we needed the manpower to stave it off, but my sense of injustice wouldn't be silent. "We can't just leave him in their hands."

Abigor's eyes lit up with fury. "We can, and we will. Those were his orders, and I will not dishonor him by disobeying."

That was the difference between us and them. They lived by a code, by orders that could not be circumvented. But the MPD ... We'd usually rather die than leave a man behind. Except this time, we had, and my stomach ached with the horror of it.

Abigor broke eye contact with me and addressed Bane. "Our defenses have been breached, our numbers are diminished. If we remain here and are attacked again, then we may not be able to fend off the shades."

Bane's jaw flexed. "Our grounds are warded,

and we have ample room in the east wing of the mansion."

Ryker's mouth turned down, and Orin's brows flicked up, but it was Cassie who spoke.

"How does it feel to need help, huh?" Her drawl had real bite.

Abigor blinked down at her in surprise. "Excuse me?"

She crossed her arms under her breasts. "You sit here in your fucking clifftop house, just watching shit go down all the time, when you have the power to help. You're lucky we didn't do the same to you."

Abigor's eyes narrowed, and his lips thinned. "Believe me, sitting back and doing nothing has been the hardest thing we've ever had to do."

Cassie frowned, confused.

They didn't know the truth about the deal between the White Wings and the Black Wings. They didn't realize that to interfere in Midnight's human affairs would mean handing humanity's free will to the White Wings. Malphas had said we weren't permitted to tell humans about the deal, but it was time the nephs found out. If we were going to work together, there had to be trust and a level of respect.

It was time to spill the beans. "Cassie, there's something you need to understand ..."

I filled her and the others in. Abigor didn't try to stop me. There were no humans nearby to eavesdrop. No live ones anyway.

"Are we winning?" Orin asked once I was done. "Which side has the most humans?"

Abigor's lip curled. "Right now, after all the humans we've lost to the shades, the White Wings are in the lead."

"Fuck!" Ryker hung his head, hands on hips.

"Yes. Fuck is the right word," Abigor said. "Because the White Wings have proven that they don't consider the shades their problem. They're just counting down the days until they can claim their prize."

"At this rate, there won't be a prize to claim," Orin pointed out.

"They have tunnel vision, and with the divine wards they've placed around Dawn, there is no way to force them to see the truth."

The truth? The truth was that in a few months the century would be up and the barriers around Arcadia would come down. The White Wings would get to claim all the humans outside of our little prison, and the shades … the shades would be free. Oh, shit. I met Abigor's eyes and saw my thoughts reflected there. He inclined his head in acknowledgement. I still hadn't forgiven him for kidnapping me from Desert Rock, but even I knew when to call a truce. The White Wings were complete idiots.

"So, what do we do?" Cassie asked.

I took a deep breath. "We do what we always do. We stop the shades from taking out any more humans. We fix this."

Bane pulled me into the lounge as soon as we entered the mansion. Ryker and Rivers made to follow, but Bane shook his head. Rivers shot me a questioning look, just the merest twitch of an eyebrow, but I knew what it meant—are you okay? Do you need me to stay?

I shook my head behind Bane's broad frame, and Rivers and Ryker backed up. Ryker didn't look too happy about it, though. My about-to-fall-flat-on-my face sway probably didn't help much. Bane slid the lounge doors closed and then headed straight for the drinks tray.

My feet made a beeline for the wingback, and my ass thanked them as soon as it touched leather. Bane handed me a huge measure of whiskey, and I took a large gulp, coughing half the liquid up when it went down the wrong way. Urgh.

Bane patted me on the back none too gently.

I ducked away from him. "Easy. Shit, do you want me to cough up my lungs too?"

He backed up. "Dammit, Harker. Be careful."

He pinched the bridge of his nose.

"I'm fine." But a peek from beneath my lashes showed that *he* wasn't. "I guess you want the full scoop, right?"

He crossed his epic arms across his equally epic chest and tucked in his chin. "You were in contact with Xavier for long enough to take him out. Why didn't you?" His eyes narrowed. "You can't let the host body deter you, Harker. Drayton is gone."

The fact that he was referring to Drayton as Xavier, his shade name, and the fact that he'd called Drayton the *host body*, wasn't lost on me. It was his way of mentally distancing himself from the fact that his closest friend was now a vessel for a shade. It was what I'd been doing too, except Bane didn't know that. It didn't stop a spark of anger from flaring to life in my chest, though.

I placed my glass on the table and stood up. "If anyone knows what's at stake here, it's me. If anyone feels the burden of what's happening, it's me. *I* chose to rip open that veil. *I* let the fuckers out. *I* tried to expel Xavier. But it didn't work, and I was about to kill him, but he told me Drayton was still inside, still holding on."

His brows shot up and then came down in a look I recognized as his damn-Harker-you're-a-fool look. "And you believed him."

"No. Of course not." I licked my suddenly dry lips. "I delved deeper and I saw for myself."

Bane's breathing quickened. "You saw? Drayton is alive?"

I nodded. "I saw his light. He's still there, Bane. We can save him. We have to."

Bane began to pace. "But you *couldn't* expel Xavier. If you can't expel him, or kill him without killing Drayton, then there *is* nothing we can do."

"I think the shades have a power hierarchy of their own. I think the ones I've come up against are lower-level. Most of them have taken minor nephs and humans. But I saw a Lupin there tonight."

He looked up sharply. "I saw two. No Sanguinata, though."

"I think the more powerful the shade, the more powerful the host it can claim."

"Makes sense." Bane rubbed his chin.

Now was my cue to tell him the rest, and my stomach turned. "There's more …"

He met my gaze and his expression softened. "Harker, whatever it is, you can tell me."

"If Drayton is still lingering after all this time, then maybe other nephs who've been infected are also still inside their bodies. Trapped. Still alive. We just assumed that if they were attacking us, then, like the humans, their souls must be gone. But Cassie managed to hold on for weeks." I wrung my hands. "I think by killing the shades, I've also been killing nephs."

Bane closed his eyes. "Fuck."

My stomach flipped and a queasy sensation filled me. "I can't risk it anymore. I can't kill until I've checked for the soul."

Bane tilted back his head. There was silence for a long minute as he thought things through. "There won't always be time to check. In the heat of battle, you need to do what you must to eliminate the threat. You could risk your life and find out the neph soul is too far gone. They could die anyway." He looked at me steadily, his violet eyes gleaming in the firelight. It was his I've-come-to-a-decision face, which usually ended in an order. "If you get a shot, Harker, you take it. No checking for souls. That's an order."

He was *ordering* me to knowingly kill innocents? "No. I can't. I won't."

"Yes, you will."

Impotent anger surged up my throat, robbing me of a constructive sentence. "Fuck you, Bane."

He strode toward me and gripped my arms, lifting me off my feet slightly. "Don't get it twisted, Harker. I may want you. I may enjoy you, and I may feel things for you that drive me crazy, but you are *not* my equal. I'm your fucking boss, and when I give an order, I expect it to be followed."

His face was a contorted mask of rage. A vein pulsed at the base of his throat, and his eyes were bloodshot and crazy. Fear—visceral and real— tightened my vocal cords, even though my brain whispered that he was afraid for me—afraid that I would get hurt if I didn't follow his ridiculous order.

The door slid open behind me, and Bane's gaze slipped over my head. "Get out." He bit the words like they were ice chips.

"I will. But I'm taking her with me." Rivers's tone was cold and measured. "Put her down, Bane." This was a new voice, the one I'd heard in the lair, the voice of the Mind Reaper.

Shit. My vocal paralysis evaporated. "Bane. You need to put me down."

Bane blinked and looked at me. His gaze flickered over to his hands biting into my flesh. His mouth softened, and he slowly peeled his fingers from my shoulders. My boots hit the ground. His expression shuttered, and he took a step away from me, as if worried about tempting fate. "Get some rest, Harker. We'll speak about this tomorrow."

In all the months I'd known him, I'd never lost sight of what he was, who he was, but it had been a while since he'd reminded me, and my legs couldn't get me out of there quick enough.

Rivers had left me at my door, even though his body language had told me it was the last thing he'd wanted to do. Fucked up how I could read them all so easily now. A quick shower washed away the shitty feeling and soothed the bruises blooming on my skin—the reminders of battle.

I stared at my reflection in the misted mirror, hair wet and stuck to my scalp, face beaded with moisture, fresh from the shower. How could I look so normal? How could I look so unaffected after everything that had happened in the early hours of this morning? It was almost seven a.m. and every inch of me screamed for bed, but my mind was a jumble of possibilities.

I'd caused this mess by ripping into the veil with my daggers, and the decision to deal with Asher and the shades without causing panic had been unanimous at the MPD. We'd voted not to tell the MED or the Lupin or Sanguinata. Damn, we'd voted to keep our world in the dark while we dealt with the unknown. But Bane had put his foot down at cutting out the winged. After all, he'd reasoned, it was the winged the shades wanted dead. With the help of Ava and her unit and Marika and her Order, we'd worked round the clock to patrol and look for shade activity and stop it. But I was the only one who could see them, the only one who could hurt them. And that put us at a distinct disadvantage, not to mention how fucking sneaky they were.

This was bigger than the MPD, bigger than Black Wings versus White Wings. And yet the White Wings had put Dawn into lockdown, setting up powerful wards to keep anything and everything out. As far as we were aware, the Sanguinata hadn't been affected, but then they *were* holed up in a mansion surrounded by a moat, away from it all. Aside from The Breed leader, Max, Drayton, and Merlin, the Lupin was the first higher-tier neph to be taken. If I was right, and only the most powerful shades could take top-tier nephs as hosts, the Lupin sightings today meant more powerful shades were coming out to play. God, it all made my head hurt.

Stumbling out of the bathroom, I padded over to my bed and climbed wearily onto the mattress. The door opened softly, and someone entered, but I was damned if I was gonna lift my head or turn around to look.

The bed dipped and then heat brushed against my arm. I breathed in, cinnamon and spice, and smiled. "Snuggles?"

Ryker pulled me into his arms. "You fucking bet."

I sighed as his chest pressed against my back, as his thighs brushed the back of mine.

I chuckled. "You should just move in. How many nights is that this week?"

"I don't hear you complaining."

I relaxed into his embrace. "That's because I'm not. I mean it. You should just move in."

He kissed the top of my head and inhaled. "It wouldn't be fair."

"Fair? On who?"

His sigh tickled the back of my head. "It doesn't matter."

Realization dawned … he was referring to the others, to Orin and Rivers and Bane. It wouldn't be fair to them if Ryker took up residence in my room.

"You could have died today," he said softly. "Asher could have killed you."

"I know." I laced my fingers through his and closed my eyes.

"One moment you were by my side and then the next you were gone. I couldn't find you. I searched and searched and you were gone." His voice cracked.

I squeezed his hand. "I'm okay. Everything is okay."

He tucked in his chin, rubbing his face against the back of my neck, and then his lips found my nape in a soft kiss. My stomach flipped hard, and I was suddenly wide awake, mouth dry and heart beating just a little bit too fast.

He'd never touched me like this before, kissed me like this … This felt intimate in a new way to what *we* were about. Out of everyone here, I was closest to Ryker, most intimate with him in thought and emotion. With Ryker, I opened up and truly let my guard down. He was my friend ... I should pull away and put distance between us. As if sensing my thoughts, he tensed and then relaxed his hold, giving me an out.

Letting go would be a signal for him to leave, and that was the last thing I wanted. I squeezed his hand instead. "Sleep with me tonight?"

He exhaled slow and even, and then his body relaxed against mine, and he pulled me close. "Snuggles?"

"Hell, yeah."

Sharing a bed with Ryker always gave me the best night's sleep, so it was with a bounce in my step, several hours later, that I entered the kitchen to find Marika and Ava huddled over mugs of coffee. They yawned in unison and then both burst into exhausted laughter.

"You guys need to sleep." I snagged a mug and emptied the remains of the coffee pot into it.

"I *have* been sleeping," Ava said. "Loads. It just doesn't seem to be enough."

"Me too," Marika said with another yawn. She laid her head on the table. "I could sleep right now."

"Tell that to the luggage under your eyes, ladies." I popped the biscuit tin on the table. "Eat something sugary. It'll give you a boost."

"Do we have chocolate?" Ava dived in.

Marika perked up. "Did someone say chocolate?"

I grinned. "Not in that tin but ..." I walked over

to the cupboard where the stash of fancy chocolate biscuits were hidden. The ones Bane and I loved. "I'm gonna share these once." I opened a packet and set it on the table. "Just this once, okay?"

Ava was already munching and Marika joined in a moment later, sighing with pleasure.

I picked one up and dunked it in my coffee. "Good, huh?"

"Sooo good," Ava said around a mouthful.

The chair scraped on the ground as I pulled it out. "You guys ready for the meeting later?"

"I think we should be asking you that question," Marika said.

My tummy fluttered. "As ready as I'll ever be."

All eyes would be on me once Bane revealed what I could do. The pressure would be magnified tenfold, and I'd be held accountable. I'd had a choice—let Ryker be killed or let more monsters into our world. I'd saved my friend, and not everyone would applaud me for that, especially now that I was failing at fixing what I'd broken.

Boot falls echoed down the stairs leading to the kitchen and Orin's huge frame entered. His brows flicked up at the sight of us, and then he smiled and it was as if the sun had come out to play. Damn. Where had that corny thought come from?

"Ladies," he said in the smooth, sexy drawl of his. One he probably didn't even know he had. "Is this a private meeting or can anyone join in?"

Ava kicked out a chair. "Take a pew, Handsome."

He grinned, and the tips of his ears grew pink. Aw, man, could he get any sweeter? It was rare these days that I saw him without Cassie close behind, so it was nice to have him all to myself … I mean, to share him with Ava and Marika. The feminine click of boots cut off my thoughts, and Cassie appeared in the doorway. She took in the scene—Orin surrounded by females—and her expression darkened, but then she caught my eye, and she plastered a smile on her face.

"Coffee meeting?" she said brightly.

"Totally impromptu," Ava said before shoving another biscuit in her mouth.

Cassie slid into the seat beside Orin and slipped her arm through his. I tore my gaze away and fixed it on my mug. They were together. She was allowed to touch him. I wasn't.

"Are you okay?" Orin said.

Ava nudged me. Oh, he was talking to me. I glanced up and nodded. "Yeah, fine."

He swallowed. "Good. I was worried about you after everything that happened at the clifftop house." His gaze darkened. "You could have been killed."

"But she wasn't," Cassie pointed out. Her fingers flexed on his arm. "She's fine." Her smile, like her voice, was too bright.

What had happened to the confident, kick-ass woman I'd met when I'd arrived? This post-shade woman was clingy and insecure, and could I really blame her? She probably sensed the pull between Orin and me, because it was still there, despite him having made the decision to be with Cassie. That attraction and the need to be in each other's orbit hadn't evaporated. It was why I'd avoided him as much as possible without being obvious about it— avoided *them*.

"I'm fine." My smile was reassuring. "I slept really well when I finally got into bed."

"With Ryker," Orin said.

I blinked at him. "Um, yeah. Ryker kept me company."

Ava turned in her seat with a filthy smirk. "I didn't know you and Ryker were a thing. He is hawt."

My neck heated. "We're not. It's not like that with us. He just held me while I slept." Okay, it sounded weird when said out loud, but fuck it, I didn't need to explain my relationships to anyone.

"How did *you* know she was with Ryker?" Cassie asked Orin.

He blinked and looked down at her, as if noticing her presence for the first time. "What?"

"How did you know Ryker was in bed with her?"

"I went to check on Serenity last night. She was already asleep with Ryker."

Cassie slid her hand off Orin's bicep, and he frowned in confusion. Marika and Ava exchanged glances then ducked their heads. I couldn't tear my gaze away from Orin's perplexed face. He'd come to check up on me in the middle of the night. He'd come to my bedroom without telling his girlfriend. And he didn't see what was wrong with that? Oh man, sweet Orin, with a pure heart and no clue. And now Cassie was looking at him as if he'd just told her he'd strangled her pet dog.

Orin cocked his head. "Cassie?"

"Wow," she said. "You really don't see what you did wrong, do you?"

His brow furrowed. "I went to check on a

friend. What's wrong with that?" There was a definite bite to his tone now.

"You went to another woman's bedroom in the middle of the night without telling me," she said slowly, as if explaining something to a child.

I had to give Orin props—he kept his cool. "Another *woman*? It's Serenity, not some random female."

But that was the whole point for Cassie. If Orin were my boyfriend I'd be pissed too, but this wasn't a discussion that should be open viewing. They needed their privacy, and if they weren't going to take it elsewhere then I'd make myself scarce.

I drained my coffee and pushed back my chair. "I'll see you guys in a couple of hours."

I headed out of the kitchen and up the stairs. The scrape of more seats followed as Ava and Marika had the same idea, but I didn't wait for them to catch up. I needed to be on my own, and there was only one place where I knew I wouldn't be disturbed.

The roost.

Half an hour in the chilly air and my pulse had returned to normal. It didn't mean anything that Orin had come to check up on me, not to him. He'd come as a friend, but then there'd been that flash of jealousy in his eyes when he'd mentioned finding me with Ryker. That query in his tone. No. I was imagining things. He loved Cassie and cared for me, and that was it. I needed to move on and forget we'd ever been close. We'd agreed to be friends and not avoid each other, but over the past few weeks being in his company and having to hold back from touching him had been torture. I wouldn't have thought twice about it before Cassie came back, but now, with her watching me like a hawk, knowing that I felt more than friendship for him, every tactile moment felt wrong. And now, with him having admitted he'd come to my room late at night, she'd be watching me even more closely. Urgh. I was greedy, that's what I was. No matter how moral or good I wanted to be, there was the dark kernel of covetousness that unfurled inside me when it came to the guys. They weren't mine, and yet it felt as if they were.

No, we are cambion, my daimon reminded me gently. *Do not shy away from what we are and what we need. Do not explain away our emotions, for we feel more than others.*

Leaving the roost, I headed down the stone steps to the main house. The thud of boots echoed up toward me and then Orin appeared on the steps below.

"Serenity." He hovered, looking suddenly uncertain.

Had he been about to come to the roost? Shit. No one but Bane and I went there. He must be desperate to see me. Ignoring the stab of hope, I composed my features. "What's up?"

"I wanted to apologize for earlier."

I shrugged. "There's nothing to apologize for."

He sighed. "Yes, there is. Cassie made you feel uncomfortable. Heck, she made me feel bad for a second. But I refuse to apologize for caring."

It wouldn't be right to pretend that Cassie was in the wrong. "She had a point, Orin. You're her boyfriend. You made a commitment to her, and coming to my room that late at night … it just sends the wrong message. I'd be pissed too if I were Cassie."

He took another step toward me. "I came to check on you because you almost died, and I was worried. I'd do it again if need be, and if you need someone to hold you at night and Ryker can't be there, then I'd fill in, in a heartbeat."

My pulse skipped, and I swallowed hard. "Orin, you can't do that." Dammit, where was the certainty in my tone. "You can't say that. Cassie is your girlfriend." The final words were delivered with more conviction.

His expression hardened. "And I've told her that if she wants us to work, she needs to accept how important *you* are to me."

My stomach flipped. "What? Why? I mean, how?" Dumb question, but my mouth was on autopilot.

He smiled softly. "It was easy, I just opened my mouth and the words fell out."

What was he doing? "I don't want to come between you two. If you want your relationship with Cassie to work, then you can't put me first."

His brow furrowed and his fists clenched. "I can't fight my instincts on this."

My throat was suddenly dry as sand. He ducked his head. Yeah, cue awkward moment, but that was something I could defuse.

I punched him lightly on the shoulder.

"Friendship can be like that. I'm glad ours is safe, but you need to work harder on things with Cassie if you want it to work out."

He met my eyes, his expression sober, and reached up to cup my cheek with his warm hand. "Nothing will ever come in the way of our friendship. You've been there for me every time I've needed a shoulder to cry on. You've stood up for me when I've been unable to do so for myself. I know things are confusing right now. I know you have Bane and Rivers and you've gotten close. I know how much you care for Ryker and how much you mean to him, but I want you to know, I'm here for you too. Always. Cassie is just gonna have to deal with that."

He just wasn't listening to me. He wasn't even listening to himself. If he felt this way, then why stay with her? Was it guilt at not figuring out that Cassie was infected? Did he blame himself for leaving her in the shade's clutches? Did he believe that he owed it to her to be with her? It wasn't my place to point any of this out. He needed to figure it out for himself; besides, his words were doing strange things to my tear ducts.

"Is this our cue to hug?" I arched a brow, trying to mask the churning emotions inside me.

He held out his arms. "You know it."

I leaned into his embrace and allowed him to wrap me in his sea breeze aroma. Man, there was nothing like an Orin hug. The guy was a master.

We broke apart a moment later. "Come on. Let's go find Bane and get the details on the meeting."

"Already did that," Orin said.

"And?"

"We're meeting everyone at The Deep."

My brows shot up. "Dorian agreed to come to The Deep?"

Orin nodded.

"Dorian, as in, I'm-the-greatest, suck-on-my-cock, Dorian? Dorian who thinks he's Sanguinata royalty, Dorian?"

Orin chuckled. "And you call me a poet."

I linked arms with him and tugged him down the steps. "Now this I have to see."

The Deep had been locked down for our meeting. Signs had been erected stating that the place had been hired for a private party. Not really a party, but it would keep out everyone who didn't need to be in the know. We'd agreed that the Black Wings should stay out of it on this occasion; there was way too much animosity toward them, and their presence would just rile the nephs up.

Orin and Rivers manned the doors, and I huddled in the foyer, out of the cold, sipping a hot chocolate that Jonah had whipped up for me. My stomach was a knot of nerves, and my hands were ice blocks. What if things got ugly? It was a possibility, of course. No one liked being kept in the dark. Our intentions had been noble, but still … Maybe it hadn't been a good idea to keep quiet about the shades.

"Too late to worry about that now," Bane said, coming up behind me.

His huge hands closed over my shoulders, channeling his warmth into my blood. My body instinctively leaned into him, wanting to revel in the heat of his abdomen against my back, but we still had some issues to clarify, so I pulled away and turned to face him.

He exhaled sharply through his nose. "I was worried about you. I lost it. But I would never have hurt you. I didn't hurt you … did I?" His face twisted into an expression that was part fear, part pain.

Damn him for getting in there quick with an apology. And sincere too. But still. We needed some ground rules. "No. You didn't hurt me. But it wasn't pleasant. I get that you were worried. But I won't allow you to manhandle me like that. It can't happen again."

He closed his eyes and breathed deep and even. "It won't. You have my word."

I smiled sweetly and leaned up to press a kiss to his cheek. "Good. And from now on, if you want to play boss, you can do it in the bedroom. Otherwise, we're on equal terms."

"What? No." He was looking at me as if I'd told him I could fart the alphabet.

Heck yes. "*I'm* the one with the power to kill the shades. *I'm* the one with the power to expel them, and *I'm* the one putting myself on the front line, so I get an equal say. You do *not* get to order me. We discuss and we decide, together. Got it?"

His chest rumbled in a suppressed growl and the hairs on the back of my neck stood to attention. I was prodding the beast, but it had to be done. There was no backing down. Not from this.

He looked over my head, his expression flat. "You act with your heart, not with your head."

"I will not kill innocents just to save time."

"Every moment you spend searching an infected host for a soul is a moment that the shade can break free and kill you."

He was right, but … "I will not kill innocents to save time."

"Damn you, woman."

Wait for it …

"You will work fast, and you will have one of us by your side at all times."

And that was the ticket. "Deal." I grinned up at him.

He leaned down so his lips brushed the delicate shell of my ear. "And later tonight I will be playing a very bossy boss."

His hot breath sent a lance of lust straight to the juncture of my thighs. I swallowed hard. "I'll be there."

Rivers strode over to us, his lean body weaving through the crowd. When had that happened? When had everyone arrived?

Bane's lips twitched. Smug bastard. He knew he could make the world melt away with a touch.

"Is everyone in position?" he asked Rivers, never taking his smoldering gaze off me.

Right now I didn't *need* to feed, but damn, I *wanted* to.

"Yes," Rivers said. "We have officers all around the room; they're armed. Marika and her people are settling in the crowd to help defuse tension if need be."

It was all we could do. If anyone kicked off, then we'd have to deal with it, but we were going to be speaking to the Sanguinata and the Lupin, and they were big on order, so here was to hoping that they kept their cool. If anyone was going to get difficult, it would be Langley and his MED buddies.

As if summoned by my thoughts, the Sanguinata entered The Deep led by Dorian, their self-proclaimed illustrious leader. He was dressed in a crimson silk shirt and smart black slacks. His hair was brushed back from his high forehead, nostrils slightly flared as if he'd just smelled something bad. Urgh. My hand already itched to slap him, and he hadn't even opened his mouth to speak yet. He caught my eye and his lip curled slightly in a mocking smile. He inclined his head and arched a brow, and I swear I chucked up a little bit in my mouth.

The bloodsucking wanker took a step toward me, and Bane's hand spread across my lower back, steadying and reassuring.

"Dorian, thank you for coming," Bane said.

Rivers stepped up to my right and crossed his arms.

Dorian didn't come any closer. "Well, color me intrigued. Look at all the nephs come out to play." He raised his head and inhaled. "And humans too?" He arched a brow. "You're providing snacks?"

My smile was saccharine. "If you want your snacks to stab you in the throat, then yeah, try your luck. All the humans here are trained in combat. They're an extension of the MPD."

Not Langley, of course. Everyone knew the MED head, and they wouldn't dare harm him, not without risking epic repercussions. The man in question was already here, standing by the bar, whiskey in hand, stone-cold gaze scraping the floor.

His lips were turned down, making it clear he was *not* happy to be here.

Dorian moved off with his lackeys but hovered close by, within earshot no doubt. Gregory, the leader of the Lupin pack, was next to saunter in. Unlike Dorian, who sent others into battle in his name, Gregory fought for the causes he believed in. After the Lupin's assistance on our last scourge attack, which had turned out to be an ambush, I had a serious soft spot for the hairy wolf-man.

He cut his way through the crowd, past humans and Sanguinata, and made a beeline for me.

A smile crinkled his eyes. "It's good to see you again, Harker."

"You too, Gregory. Clothes suit you."

Rivers made a choked sound. But Gregory was unperturbed.

He grinned. "And I can honestly say I believe that you'd look better without yours."

Bane's hand was still hovering on my back, and his fingers flexed against my flesh at Gregory's words.

My neck heated, but I kept my composure and matched his grin. "Always the charmer."

He gave me a mock bow.

"Thank you for coming at such short notice, Gregory." Bane's tone was deliberately polite.

If Gregory noticed the tepid tone, he didn't show it. If anything, his smile widened. He jerked his chin up at Bane and then walked off toward the bar. Three Lupin I didn't recognize trailed after him. Their gait was relaxed and loping, but it was a deception, because these loose-limbed creatures were killers in human skin. In fact, we were surrounded by killers. If things went sour … No. Not thinking about that.

"It's time," Bane said.

My stomach fluttered then did an acrobatic flip. "I'm ready."

But I so wasn't.

Rivers cleared a path to the bar, where a pedestal had been placed to accommodate me, and I took my spot. Damn, now I could see everyone. All the faces and eyes and shit. Focus on one thing, one point. One person. I found Ryker and Orin. Yeah, I'd alternate between the two. This could work.

"Hey!" Bane clapped his hands, his voice a boom.

The murmuring cut off and all eyes were on me. Shit. This was my cue. Bane and Rivers flanked me while Ryker and Orin stood at the head of the crowd, their expressions reassuring.

I licked my lips. "Thank you all for coming today. Some of you may have noticed a change in the atmosphere of Midnight over the past few weeks. You may have felt a dark presence, the feeling that something was coming?"

Silence.

I cleared my throat. "Okay, well something *did* come. Something entered our world two weeks ago, and we need your help to stop it."

The silence that greeted me was loaded, but before anyone could exclaim or ask a question I launched into my mentally prepared speech, starting with Cassie's infection and ending with the battle at the clifftop mansion. Ryker held my gaze throughout, his expression tight. He was nervous on my behalf, and the urge to protect him surged up, giving me confidence and making the words come smooth and easy.

Finally, everything they needed to know was out there, on the table. "So, we need your help. We need to find a way to stop the shades from taking hosts. We need your help to fight them."

It was Langley who broke the crowd's silence. "And you tell us this *now*?" He stepped forward, drink in hand. "Have you any idea how many fucking missing persons reports we've been flooded with? Do you realize how rammed the psych ward is with people complaining about hearing voices? Have you even the slightest inkling how many people suffering from anemia symptoms, with no actual iron deficiency, are in the hospital right now? And it's all connected to the shit you brought into our world."

My heart beat faster. This was to be expected, this outburst and the shit he was saying. We'd had no clue about the sick humans. "I'm sorry. I honestly thought we could contain the problem."

Langley made a disgusted sound. "You shouldn't have let them in. You had a choice and you made the wrong call. Fucking mystical daggers shouldn't have chosen you. It's you fucking supernaturals that have made Midnight hell."

"Whoa!" Ava stepped forward. "If it wasn't for the MPD most of us would have been killed by the rippers and suckers by now."

Langley opened his mouth to argue, but Gregory butted in. "You have our help. Whatever you need. This affects us all. Midnight is our home, and we won't have some fuckers tear it apart with a petty grudge against the winged. Trust me, if they wanted to go straight for the winged and be done with it, I'd step back and watch, but several of my Lupin have gone missing, and now I know who's responsible. I will not stand by and let them get away with it."

The knot of tension that had formed in my chest eased a bit. We had the Lupin on our side.

"Langley?" Bane asked. "Can we count on MED aid?"

Langley cursed under his breath. "Not like we have much choice. Humans are being targeted. We have to do something." He shot me a lethal look.

I deserved it. This was on me, so I'd let him have this time to vent, but after today, if he said a negative word about it, I'd be delivering a smackdown.

I looked to Dorian. The Sanguinata were many, they were powerful if they chose to get off their arses and actually do something, and I was pretty sure that their stronghold contained a mini arsenal.

Dorian ran his tongue over his teeth. He was savoring the moment. Reveling in the attention. "You say the shades latch onto shadows? Human and neph?"

I nodded. "Yes. That seems to be how they infect their hosts."

He smiled smugly. "Well then, the Sanguinata are immune to attack. We don't have shadows."

The crowd erupted into conversation. Bane clapped his hands again, calling for quiet, but my mind was reeling, making connections and churning up possibilities.

Dorian shrugged. "I guess we'll see you all

when this is over." He turned to leave.

"Wait!"

He paused and glanced over his shoulder. "What now? Are you going to beg?" He rolled his eyes. "Please don't. It will ruin the dominatrix vision of you that I've developed for my viewing pleasure."

Bane growled low and menacing, and Dorian's eyes flared in panic.

I placed a hand on Bane's shoulder, keeping my attention on Dorian. "No. No begging. Just a little insight. Tell me, what are you going to do once the shades have taken over all the humans in Midnight?"

Dorian blinked at me.

"You know, once your food supply and all the humans who are part of your House have been infected? What are you going to do for food?"

The realization was a ripple of emotions skating across Dorian's face, and yeah, there was no stopping the stab of satisfaction that shot through me. I had him, and he knew it. He canted his head as if reconsidering. Like he actually had any other options.

"Of course the humans under our protection are important to us," he said in a smooth and smarmy tone. "We have an obligation to them." He gave me a closed-lipped smile. "We will do what we can for the humans. All humans under our protection will be offered sanctuary on Sanguinata grounds."

"Like hell!" Ryker took the words right out of my mouth.

I crossed my arms. "You don't exactly have a stellar track record when it comes to hospitality to humans. I doubt any human would like to play sippy cup to a Sanguinata."

His eyes narrowed to slits. "Then what *do* you want?"

It was my turn to smile, but I gave him the full benefit of my even white teeth. "I want you to lend us soldiers. We need boots on the ground, and you have plenty to spare."

He sighed. "Very well. You will have your men. But how will that prevent these shades from infecting humans? What are you going to do about that?"

It wouldn't, but my subconscious had found a possible solution. "We need to give the humans and other nephs the same advantage as the Sanguinata. We need to find a way to get rid of our shadows. Some arcane magic, some ritual, some spell—there has to be a way to strip us of our shadows."

"That's ridiculous!" Langley's previously disgruntled expression was now incredulous. "You can't strip people of their shadows. Shadows aren't a *thing* you can take away. Shadows are cast when light falls on an object—in our case, moonlight."

"I know how shadows are formed, Langley, and yet Sanguinata don't cast them." I arched a brow. "Which tells me there is more to shadows than we realize."

He opened and closed his mouth a couple of times, then settled for curling his lip. Man, he really didn't like me.

A low murmur flitted over the gathered. I looked for Marika, but she was whispering with one of her Order buddies. Was there a solution? I'd seen the shades latch on to humans' shadows the day they'd poured into our world. The moon had been huge and bright that night. They'd merged into darkness and then been swallowed up somehow, becoming one with the human. This had to be their way in. If we could get rid of our shadows, then maybe we could stop the shades from gaining access to our bodies.

"Marika?" I waved to get her attention.

She looked up, a frown etched on her face.

"Is it possible? Do you think there's a way to do that?"

Marika winced. "We're still learning how to manipulate the arcane, and there is so much we still don't know."

"So … Not *impossible*, as far as you're aware."

"No. But … it's a mighty long shot, and the texts we need are back at the Order."

"Shit."

She held up her hand. "Leave it to us. We'll sort it. If it can be done, then we'll find a way."

It *was* a long shot, but the hope had given everyone a boost, and the conversation that broke out now was excited and optimistic.

"What about all the sick people?" Langley asked. "Could they all be infected?"

Shit. The ones in the psych ward probably were. "I'll drop in at the hospital and check everyone out. If they are infected, then I'll expel the shades."

"Expel?" He made a disgusted face. "You need to kill them."

"If I do that, then I'll end up killing the human too. I explained that a few minutes ago."

He scratched his forehead. "Fine. Just do what you have to do to fix this."

Ryker and Orin moved off toward Gregory, probably to discuss strategy and manpower. Rivers made a beeline for Dorian, who was trying to make a hasty getaway. Bane held out his hand to help me off the platform.

Thank God the public speaking part was over.

"Marika is right. It is a long shot," Bane said, his voice low.

"I know. But we have to try. What else can we do?"

He tucked in his chin. "I don't know. Let's hit the hospital and check out the humans there. Maybe we'll get inspired."

"I love your optimism."

He responded with a snort.

Rivers joined us. "We should check out the hospital now."

"Yeah, Bane just suggested that. We're leaving in a minute."

"I'm coming with you," Rivers said. "Just spoke to Langley. The psych ward is bad, and if someone turns while you're there, then you could do with the extra backup."

That was fine by me. "Let's get this done. Those poor people have suffered enough."

The human hospital was on the other side of town, about a mile and a half from the border to Sunset. Thank goodness the shades hadn't invaded that district yet, but it was only a matter of time until they did. We needed to nip this in the bud before that could happen.

Bane drove with one hand on the wheel, his pose relaxed to the untrained eye, but the intensity of his expression and the tense thigh muscles spoke differently. It was weird, but the fact that he was stressing made me relax a little, as if by taking on the tension, he was relieving me of it.

Rivers sat in the backseat, his eyes on the road as it flew by. Silence reigned, and it should have been uncomfortable, except it wasn't. Not with these two, who only spoke when they had something to say.

The building came into view, and Bane turned into the sloping car park. Rivers jumped out to get a ticket for the van.

"You haven't fed for two weeks," Bane said, surprising me with his soft tone.

I'd hoped he wouldn't notice, then I could have pretended there was nothing wrong for a little while longer. But now that he'd mentioned it, it was impossible to ignore the itch of power under my skin. It was back again, even though I'd incinerated several shades less than twenty-four hours ago.

"I haven't needed to."

"Since when?"

"Since I unlocked this shade-killing power." I winced. "It's actually causing me a bit of discomfort."

"Explain."

"There's too much power inside. Like, I can feel it growing and the only thing that helps is killing shades. I kill, and it relieves the pressure a little. But then it's back a few hours later … I'm afraid of what will happen if I can't kill enough shades to keep the power in control." There, I'd said it.

His jaw flexed. "Why didn't you say anything sooner?"

"I was hoping it would just resolve itself. Look, we have so much other shit to deal with I didn't want to add to the pile, but it's getting worse so … yeah, now you know."

Bane sucked in his bottom lip. "Well, we best find you some shades to kill." He glanced at the hospital. "Maybe we'll get lucky."

Hope swelled and then died when guilt stabbed at it. What was I thinking? My being able to kill a shade meant that a human had already lost its soul.

Bane held my gaze. "Shelve the guilt, Harker. You die and we're all fucked. So, if it takes a human soul being devoured to keep you alive, then so be it."

Wow. Way to put things into perspective. But

despite the rough tone, his words did take the edge off the guilt just a smidge.

"Thanks."

Rivers rapped on the driver side window, and Bane rolled it down to take the ticket. It was time to do some clean-up.

"The MPD has no jurisdiction here." The receptionist at the check-in desk looked like she'd just sucked on Lilith's sour tits.

I had to give her credit though, because she didn't even flinch under Bane's fiery gaze. The woman was playing her role of gatekeeper well. The double-glazed reinforced doors to the psych ward lay to our left. No entry without being buzzed through from the inside, and to get buzzed through, this dragon had to call in using the shiny phone behind her.

"We're here to help." Bane bit out the words. "Call Langley at MED if you need confirmation."

"I'm afraid the phones can't be used to make outside calls." She crossed her arms over her scrawny chest. "You'll need to bring me a council order giving you access to the psych patients. Alternatively, you can—"

An alarm cut off her words, and a bulb fixed to the wall behind her flashed red. Screams filtered through the reinforced glass, and then the whole thing shuddered with the impact of something.

Rivers rushed to the door and peered through the round windows. "Fuck. Open the door, now!" His tone was a hot razor but still the woman faltered.

Fuck this. I pushed past her and grabbed the phone on the wall and pressed the buzzer. It rang and rang but no one answered. Meanwhile, the screams intensified.

"We need to get in there!" Rivers strode toward the woman, his face a chilly mask of threat. "There has to be an override switch out here somewhere. Show me, now!"

Another thud from beyond the doors coupled with the fact that Rivers looked like he was about to take chunks out of the woman had her scrambling for a keypad under her desk. She hit a sequence of buttons, and the doors made an audible click.

Bane yanked them open, and a body fell out. An orderly, if the uniform was anything to go by.

"Get back! Get out!" someone screamed.

But they didn't know what we did. They needed us.

"Seal those doors once we're through," Rivers said to the slack-jawed receptionist. "Do not open them until you get the say-so from her." He pointed at my face.

The woman nodded quickly, and Rivers and I ran through the doors after Bane, straight into chaos. Orderlies and doctors filled the corridors, and patients ran amok. The doors clicked shut behind us, and the lock engaged with a beep just as a man sprinted past us and slammed into them. He rebounded, hit the ground, got back up, and made another run at them.

I switched to aether-sight to see the shade that was inside. Fuck.

"Harker?" Bane took a step toward the man,

waiting for the word.

"Yeah. It's a shade. Crimson eyes."

Bane grabbed the shade in a headlock. The thing struggled, growling and grunting. This one was different. Less coherent. Less … intelligent? No time to ponder now. The power inside me surged up, drowning out my daimon. I needed to get it out, give her room to breathe. Pressing my hands to the shade's head, I expelled the power. The relief was a tingle in my limbs and a throb at my core. Fuck, that felt good. I needed more.

"Harker, over here!" Rivers called.

I turned to find him pinning another guy to the wall. Yeah, it looked like I was about to get another fix, because it looked like all the infected humans who had been held here were turning. A man in a white coat ran up to me as I finished with the big guy who'd just tackled me to the ground. Bane hauled the body off me and the doctor fell to his knees beside me.

"It's inside me. I can feel it. I can feel it. Please, help me."

Shit, he was infected. Time to switch gears. I grabbed his hands and tugged at the shade using my aether ability. The world around me greyed, and the shade's crimson eyes snarled at me. Fuck you, you don't belong here. Get the heck out! I yanked, and the shade slid free, ricocheting off the ceiling and then disappearing through the floor.

The doctor blinked at me, and then sagged in relief. "Oh, God. What was that? What was inside me?"

"A shade," Rivers said. "We'll fill you in, but—

" He grabbed at a guy making a run for the locked doors, managed to snag the back of his shirt, and brought him to the ground.

I scrambled up and reached for the shade, but Rivers blocked me with his body. "No. This one is mine."

"What do you mean?"

Bane gripped my elbow and pulled me away. "We might get answers from it, if we interrogate it."

"Interrogate?" I shook my head. "That's a human."

"No," Bane said. "It isn't. Not anymore."

He was right. The human soul was gone, evidenced by its blood-red irises. This was just a shell housing a foreign entity. "Fine."

Rivers hauled the guy up. And then decked him so hard he crumpled unconscious. "Okay, let's wrap up here."

"Shit's calming down now," Bane said. "I think you got all the infected."

"Probably, but we need to be sure." I smiled at the doctor. "Can you help us get everyone together?"

He nodded and blew out a breath, composing himself. "Yes. Yes, we can use the common room. It's large enough."

"I'll stow this one and be back," Rivers said. He threw the shade over his shoulder and strode off toward the exit.

The doctor began shouting orders to the other staff. And the rest of the patients were rounded up and urged into the common room. The power inside me was in check for now, so stepping into the psych ward lounge, I turned on my aether-sight.

Five expulsions, and I was wiped, but it wasn't over yet. We still had to check out the ward on the second floor where the patients with extreme fatigue were being treated. Remaining in aether-sight for so long had given me a headache, which would probably morph into a migraine if I used the sight again, but we were here now, and leaving without checking the other patients out would be a waste. At least the nurse manning this ward was slightly more accommodating. Probably due to the fact that the psych doctor had done us the courtesy of calling down to explain the situation before we arrived.

We weren't allowed to disturb the patients, but she accompanied me onto the ward and allowed me to walk up and down. Aether-sight back on, I ran an expert eye over each patient, all thirty of them.

Nothing.

They were clean.

Hmmm ... So, not related to the shade activity? Still, something to keep an eye on. Bane arched a brow as I rejoined him and Rivers at the desk.

"They're clean."

Bane's shoulders relaxed. "Good. Let's get back to the mansion."

"Excuse me?" the nurse asked tentatively. "You are going to stop this, aren't you?"

Ignoring the pounding in my temples, I plastered a smile on my face. "Yes. Yes, we are."

I walked away from her, my mouth tasting of lies.

The water from the shower beat against the back of my head as Bane's hands moved expertly over my slick body. My hands splayed against the tile as he gripped my hips and thrust into me from behind. The angle was just right, hitting the perfect spot to make me moan. He easily supported the weight of my lower body, adjusting me and taking me the way he liked. There was no feeding here, just a hot, desperate coupling, just the rasp of him inside me, and the pinch of his fingers on my flesh as he took what he needed and gave me what I wanted. He reached round and found my throbbing need, releasing the tension with a few expert strokes. I came hard, clenching around him and slamming my fist against the wet tiles as I rode the waves, because it wasn't stopping, *he* wasn't stopping. Lights flickered behind my eyelids as my throat constricted with the need to scream.

My moan was guttural and primal. Bane accompanied me, bucking as he came, beautiful curses falling from his lips like honey. He flattened me against the shower stall wall with his body and buried his head into the crook of my neck before using his mouth to tell me how much this meant to him. He was inside me, still hard, and fuck he was swelling, growing, ready to go again. Bring it. Please.

Back in the bedroom, still damp from the shower, I finished toweling my hair. Bane pulled on a pair of boxers, covering up his delectable arse. Damn.

"I think you staved off my migraine." I chucked my towel at him.

Bane caught it and slung it around his neck. Damn, he was glorious, naked save for his boxers. Every plane and dip of his powerful sculpted body was a joy to explore. I wanted him again already. How the heck was that possible?

He inhaled, his eyes fluttering closed for a moment, and a low growl emanated from his muscled chest. He ambled toward me and lifted me off my feet. I instinctively wrapped my legs around his waist as he carried me to the bed.

"I'm not done, Harker. I don't think I'll ever be done."

There was a double meaning in those words, but he didn't give me a chance to examine them, because that would mean opening up emotionally—something that was not a Bane trait. If I wanted to get close, it would be with him deep inside me. It would be in that moment when he was momentarily unguarded, when we were joined as one, that his eyes would say the words his lips refused to utter. It would have to be enough. For now.

I pulled on my jeans, my body pleasantly relaxed and serviced. "I'm going to check on Rivers."

Bane grabbed a T-shirt from his dresser. "I'll go."

"No. I can do it."

His shoulder muscles flexed and tensed beneath velvet skin. "You don't want to see him like that."

"If you're worried I'll be freaked out by Rivers's alter-ego, then don't be." I slipped on my boots. "The Mind Reaper is part of who he is, and I'm not running away from that. I can handle it. I was there when he tortured the Breed guy."

Bane pulled on his tee and then turned to face me. "That wasn't the Mind Reaper in action, Harker. That was just Rivers. Once you see the Mind Reaper, once you see that side of Rivers, it *cannot* be unseen."

His tone was saturated with warning. It thrummed with foreboding, teasing the fine hairs on the back of my neck to attention. Doubt flitted through my mind like a sudden fog, but visualizing Rivers's lean, intelligent face helped to blow it away. There was no room for doubt, not where Rivers was concerned. The Mind Reaper was a part of him that he despised and yearned for all at the same time. He needed me there. He needed someone to ground him, to remind him who he was and what he had to come back to.

He needed someone there.

Guilt flooded my veins, potent and punishing. "We shouldn't have let him do this alone. One of us should have been with him."

Dammit, we'd been fucking while he'd been … dammit! I had to get to him. Now.

Bane's gaze softened. "He doesn't work that way, Harker. He never has. When he's like this, all he thinks about is inflicting pain." His eyes flared in revelation. "He could hurt you."

My pulse skipped. "I can handle myself."

Bane's inner struggle played across his face in a series of ticks and the baring of fang. Letting me go, letting me do this, was going against every protective instinct in his bones. But ordering me not to would be going against our deal to be equals. It would be claiming me as a possession and disregarding how much Rivers meant to me.

"This isn't how it works, Harker," he said. "The Mind Reaper works alone."

"And how long has it been since the reaper was allowed out to play?"

Bane huffed, but canted his head in concession.

I offered him a conciliatory smile. "This is Rivers we're talking about. He's denied this side of himself for so long, to dive back in now without any backup …"

He hung his head, hands on hips. "You're right. Fucking hell."

Silence reigned for a long beat, and then he strode toward me, pulled me against him, and kissed the top of my head. "Go. Be with him, and make sure he comes back. I'm going to whip up some pancake batter. Rivers is always hungry when he … when he returns."

I peeked up at him through my lashes, resisting the urge to smooth back the tendrils of hair that had escaped the knot at the top of his head, but eager to soothe the beast and defuse the tension vibrating in his body. "Are you going to be wearing *the* apron?"

"Yes, Harker. I'm going to be wearing the apron because—"

"I know, I know." I nodded sagely. "Batter can be messy."

He snorted dryly and released me. "Go. Before I change my mind."

I pressed a kiss to his jaw and headed for the door.

"Harker?"

I turned back, hand on the doorknob.

"If he hurts you, hurt him back, and don't pull any punches, because if you do, I'll have to finish what you don't."

I exited Bane's chambers and headed toward the west wing. It was easier to get to the secret lair tunnel via the steps there. The sound of raised voices, male and female, had me backing up and taking the flight of steps up to the fourth floor where the Order was housed.

The voices grew louder.

"You think you can cop a feel?" Marika asked.

"I assure you, that was not my intention."

"What? You see me naked and you don't want to have a grope?" She sounded offended. "Why? What's wrong with me?"

I rounded the corner onto the corridor in time to see Marika flip open the towel she was wearing. She had her back to me, but I caught a good look at Malphas's face before he blanched and turned his back. Abigor chose that moment to appear behind his Black Wing friend. His brows shot up and he took a good, long look, surveying Marika from top to bottom.

"Nice work," he said. "Totally wasted on Malphas, though. He takes his divine duties a little too seriously. I, on the other hand, am no stranger to temptation." There was a decidedly wicked gleam in his eyes, and Marika must have seen it too because she covered herself pretty quickly.

"I apologize for interrupting your bathing," Malphas said. "But I heard you scream and thought you were in pain."

"Scream?" Marika asked. "I wasn't screaming, I was singing."

Abigor covered his smile with his hand. Malphas shook his head. "Well, I … I guess I was mistaken."

"You can turn around now," Marika huffed.

Malphas faced her, and as I approached, his lips curved in a welcome smile. Abigor merely inclined his head. The gleam in his eyes dissipated.

Marika glanced over her shoulder. "Shit. Sorry, was I *that* loud?"

I laughed. "Nope, I was passing and heard raised voices. But it looks like you have it under control."

Marika brushed her dark, wet hair off her face. "He just insulted my singing." She sniffed. "I'll have you know, I have perfect pitch." She spun on her heel and strode back into her room and slammed the door.

Abigor cleared his throat. "Well, she is certainly interesting. At least certain parts of her are."

Malphas shot him a disgusted look. "You're incorrigible."

I winced. "Best stay on your side of the mansion."

"I was looking for Bane, actually. We've been waiting for an update on the meeting?" His mouth turned down slightly. He wasn't happy about being left out of the loop.

They'd spent a long time hiding away, doing nothing. Everyone had thought they had it easy, but it must have been hard sitting on your hands and not acting to help the humans you'd sworn to protect. And now their leader, Abbadon, was gone. And, once again, they were forbidden to act to save him by an oath he'd made them take. The conflict, the suppressed frustration in Abigor's eyes, was a storm desperate to break. We needed to be more proactive about keeping them informed. Another pang of guilt assaulted me. Damn, I was beginning to feel like a pin cushion.

I smiled warmly. "I'm sorry. We got back not too long ago. He'll be in the kitchen now. You can catch him there."

Abigor's face relaxed. "Thank you."

"About Abbadon … Are you sure you don't want to go after him? If we can find out where Asher is holed up, then we can formulate an extraction plan."

It was Malphas who replied. "Abbadon is dead." His expression was deadpan.

"We have to believe that and focus on the human plight," Abigor said. "They are what is important."

I don't know how the Black Wings did it. There was no way I'd be able to be so stoic if someone I cared for was in Asher's clutches.

"Fine. But just so we're clear, it was you that took an oath, not me, not the MPD. So, if we get a shot at getting Abbadon back, then we're going to take it."

Malphas gave me a small smile. "Thank you."

I left them to it and headed back the way I'd come. By the time I made it into the tunnels under the mansion, my mind was firmly back on Rivers. *When he returns,* Bane had said. What a strange way of putting it. Rivers may have donned his Mind Reaper hat, but he was still Rivers, right? Then why were my palms all clammy as I pressed my hand to the super-secret MPD lair door? Yeah, we really needed to give it a better name.

The lab was wreathed in silence, the lights were dim, and the flashing buttons on the monitors and consoles stood out starkly in the gloom, reflecting off the tubular, fluid-filled containers holding the nephs in suspended animation.

No sign of Rivers.

But he was probably in the cell room where we'd held the Breed guy. A quick peek showed that room to be empty too. Hmmmm. Where the heck could he be? The other door I knew of led to the room with the dreadlocked neph. There were no other doors … or were there? Wait! I stepped into the cell room again and walked around the cages to the back of the chamber. There it was—a single, slender, unassuming door. It didn't even have a handle, so it blended seamlessly into the wall.

A hard push and I was through into the corridor beyond. Another door greeted me, this one with a palm print panel. Dammit. My palm didn't work. This had to be Rivers's domain. I knocked, lightly at first, and then harder.

Nothing.

Maybe Bane *should* have come with me. Rivers had been in Mind Reaper mode for at least three hours now. It couldn't be good for him to be locked away like this. I raised my fist to hammer on the door again, but it opened with a soft click.

Rivers stood in the doorway, a crimson-streaked cloth clutched lightly in his right hand. His fingers were stained with blood. Shit, it was even under his nails. Hadn't he said he didn't actually get his hands dirty when in reaper-mode? Hadn't he said that he made his subjects hurt themselves? But wait. That had been before he'd vowed not to use his siren ability.

"What do you want?" Rivers's voice was a rasp, as if he hadn't spoken in a while.

I tore my gaze from his guilty hands and drove it up to his face—his closed-off, cold, impassive face. His eyes were dead … flat.

"It's time to take a break." My voice quivered. Shit.

He turned away and walked back into the room. "I'm not done."

I stepped into the room after him, where the scent of copper mingled with fecal matter hit me hard, setting off my gag reflex. Covering my mouth and nose with my hand, I walked farther into the room. Not really a room, more a hole underground. It was composed of a plain stone floor and rough stone walls. No frills, aside from the shackles bolted to the wall and floor, and the silver trolley loaded with lethal-looking implements. No frills, aside from the dismembered body strewn across the flagstones. Torso and head were intact, but the limbs ... I gulped down bile.

What the fuck? What the *actual* fuck.

Rivers crouched by the torso and reached out to push his fingers into the wound left by the removal of the shade's arm. The shade's eyes fluttered open, and his mouth contorted in a desperate moan.

Pain ... it was feeling pain. I'd thought they didn't feel a thing, that the host's body was just a casing. They never seemed to show emotion when we stabbed and sliced in battle, and they healed. This one definitely wasn't healing.

Rivers didn't speak, he just poked and prodded and twisted. Ice trickled through my veins as I took a step back. Right now, I was presented with Rivers's back, which was good, because if I saw his face, if I saw the inhumanity in his eyes, then I'd lose it. I'd lose my conviction that the man I cared for was still there, and then my feet would do what they'd been longing to as soon as he'd opened the door.

They'd run.

I straightened my spine and breathed through my mouth to avoid the worst of the stench. "Did you get the information we need?"

"Yes," Rivers said.

"Then we're done here."

"Not finished yet."

"Why? We have what we need."

Rivers stood and walked over to the tray. His chest was rising and falling rapidly as he studied his implements of torture.

"Rivers?"

He turned his head to look at me and, damn, did it take every inch of my will power not to back the fuck up. Instead, I stared right back and lifted my chin. "Enough. It's enough."

His brow furrowed and then he cocked his head. "You keep calling me Rivers. But Rivers isn't here right now. This is *my* time, and I intend to utilize it."

I swallowed hard. "Okay, Mind Reaper, then."

He smiled then, wicked and beautiful and deadly. "I know about you. You're important to him."

I nodded. "And he told me about you. He told me that he didn't want to let you out to play unless absolutely necessary."

The Mind Reaper looked at the pieces of the shade tossed on the ground. "And it was necessary. This creature told me everything once he felt the slice of my blade."

My heart stalled. "So, why did you keep cutting?"

He blinked at me as if that was the stupidest question ever. "Whyever not?"

Oh, God.

The shade trapped in the body whimpered in pain. Trapped … it was trapped. Surely, if it could have left it would have. Did that mean that once a shade had control and the soul was gone, the shade was stuck within the human shell? But it still didn't explain why it hadn't healed itself.

"Please …" It was looking at me.

Rivers went back to surveying his tray of goodies. We had the information we needed. It was time to end this, but I needed to move fast. With a quick glance at Rivers, I switched to aether-sight and rushed toward the shade. My hand touched his flesh and the divine power rose up on instinct to tear through the shade's essence, leaving nothing but the ashes of ember. They rained down on me and clung to my lashes. And then I was hauled back by the hair and flung against the wall. My head smacked against stone and stars lit up the room. Mind Reaper didn't give me the chance to recover. His hand closed around my throat and began to squeeze.

Rivers's grip tightened. I dug my nails into his skin and twisted, but he didn't even flinch. In fact, his eyes lit up, and his mouth twisted in that sadistic smile of his.

"You interfered. No one interferes and lives."

"Rivers …" I choked out his name. "Stop." My vision was darkening. "I don't want … hurt you."

I couldn't breathe. He was taking his time, choking me by degrees to prolong my pain and his pleasure. Because there was no doubt in my mind that he was enjoying this. Damn him, he'd been warned. My daimon was on it before I could consciously decide to act. She pulled power from him, sharp and urgent. His grip loosened a fraction. It was enough for me to jerk free. But there would be no fighting him, not without hurting him. Not without getting hurt. There was only one way to pull Rivers back into the driver's seat. I needed to remind him who he was, and what he meant to me.

I grabbed Mind Reaper's face and kissed him. He resisted at first, his fingers digging into my arms as he tried to pry me off. But it was time to play parasitic leech. I kissed and fed, kissed and fed. And slowly, Rivers's body relaxed, his grip morphed from biting to a caress, and then his lips began to move against mine. I was shoved back against the wall, but this time with violent passion. His hands tangled in my hair, his tongue rasped against mine. Our teeth clashed and then he bit my lip, drawing blood, coppery but sweet. He sucked on it, tugging a moan that rose up from the depths of my core. Desire flooded my limbs. This was crazy. There was a dismembered body in the room with us.

He broke the kiss long enough to say my name and then his hand slipped between us to fumble with the buttons of my jeans. I was going to let him. I wanted him to. But not here. Not like this.

"Rivers." I pushed at his shoulders. "Rivers. No."

He froze at the word and raised his head. His dazed gaze cleared, and he blinked several times until his pale eyes were sharp and lucid once more. His mouth parted in an 'o' and then he leapt away from me as if he'd been scalded.

He stood hands on head, fingers threaded through his short silver locks as he took in the carnage.

"This is real." His voice was hoarse.

"It's okay. You're okay."

His attention snapped from the body to me, and then back again. "You saw that? Saw me do that?"

"It wasn't you. It was *him*."

He grabbed my arm and ushered me out the door into the corridor. "You have to go. Now."

I resisted. "Rivers, let me help you."

His mouth tightened and his eyes hardened. "No, Harker. Don't you get it? There *is* no helping me."

He slammed the door in my face.

I pressed a hand to the metal. He thought he was doomed, that he was a slave to the Mind Reaper … but he wasn't. Because when I'd called, he'd come back. He'd resurfaced for *me*. And there was no way I was ever going to let him lose himself like that again.

Bane had his back to me, flipping pancakes like a pro, when I entered. Ryker was nursing a cup of coffee at the table. The aroma of cinnamon laced the air, and my stomach growled.

Ryker spotted me and his face broke into a smile, but then his gaze dropped to my throat and the smile evaporated. "What the fuck happened to your neck?"

I reached up to touch my throat. What? Oh, shit. Rivers. Of course.

Bane's shoulders flexed and tensed beneath his shirt. He carefully set down the skillet and switched off the gas. And then he turned to face me, his attentions zeroing in on my throat. His jaw flexed and then he strode straight toward me. No. Not toward me. His attention was on the door. He was headed for the fucking exit.

"Ryker!" I leapt at Bane, grabbing him around the waist and holding on for dear life while using every ounce of my body weight to try and stall him, but he was still moving.

Ryker was frozen in his seat, probably wondering what the fuck was going on.

"He's going for Rivers. Help me stop him."

Ryker jumped up and grabbed Bane in a bear hug, pinning his arms to his torso.

"Get the fuck off me, Ryker." Bane's tone was a low, menacing rumble.

"Harker, what the fuck is going on?" Ryker asked.

But I was focused on Bane, on calming the monster inside. "It's okay. I'm okay. Rivers is back. He didn't let the Reaper hurt me. I'm fine. Now, please. Calm the fuck down."

"Wait. Rivers did that?" Ryker asked.

"He wasn't himself."

But Ryker was no longer listening. In fact, he was no longer holding onto Bane. Shit, he was already at the door.

Dammit. I released Bane, but slammed a hand onto his chest, then grabbed a fistful of Ryker's T-shirt. "Will you just stop, for fucksake. You can't get mad at him for what the Mind Reaper did. How does that even make sense when we allowed him to let the fucker out in the first place?"

Ryker's shoulders sagged, and the tension in the room dropped several notches.

A look at Bane's face told me he was working on cooling down too. "We good?"

He exhaled, releasing the remnants of his rage. "Yeah, Harker, we're good."

My hand slid from his chest and Ryker got the rest of his shirt back. "Now, let's have some pancakes."

Bane reached for my neck and ran a finger along the bruising. "He is so fucking lucky you're okay."

"I'm not okay, because you're starving me." I smiled and his shoulders relaxed.

"Sit." He pointed at the nearest seat.

Crisis over. For now.

We were tucking into maple syrup-covered deliciousness when Rivers finally joined us. His face was pale, his eyes haunted.

"It's done," he said before lowering himself into the nearest chair.

His hair was wet and he smelled like citrus. My gaze dropped to his hands—clean, blood-free hands. Even the nails had been scrubbed. He looked as composed and dispassionate as ever. Rivers was back in the driver's seat, and the Reaper was in lockdown. My heart ached for him. How could he live like this?

Bane jerked his head toward me. "Have you seen Harker's throat?"

Rivers blinked slowly and then looked at me, at my neck. His throat bobbed. "I did that."

It wasn't a question, but it needed an answer. "No, Rivers. You didn't. *He* did."

Rivers flinched and his pale eyes darkened. It was a crack in his armor. I'd made that crack. My pulse thrummed at the base of my throat at the revelation that I could get under his skin, under that steel persona that kept the world out. But it was gone too soon, and the shields were back up.

"Are there any more pancakes left?" he asked.

Bane scraped back his seat and donned his

apron. "I'll make you some. Plenty of batter left." He set to work at the cooker. "What did you find out?"

Rivers sat back in his seat and closed his eyes. Was he about to take a nap? I looked to Ryker, but the neph was focused on Rivers, and then the siren began to speak.

"The shade was a grunt. He didn't know too much. Just that his companions are desperate for more human hosts. He said that the humans of Midnight are hard to claim, their minds are strong. He also mentioned something about an advantage, about there being help to weaken the humans, but he didn't know what that was. Just something he'd overheard. He wasn't one of the shades in the know. He did confirm the existence of a power hierarchy among the shades, though, much like the hierarchy of an army. There are grunts and lieutenants, generals and a commander. The higher up in the ranks a shade is, the stronger they are. They can claim a powerful host. They definitely need shadows to claim a host, so we were right about that. Also, the winged can't be taken as hosts. He didn't know why, though. Just that it wasn't possible. His language skills were limited. He said something about our world being their home. About being the shepherds of God. But it didn't make sense. He also mentioned prisons. But that's all I could understand."

There was another thing gnawing at me. "Why couldn't he heal? And why didn't he just leave the body?"

He opened his eyes and looked straight at me, and the image of that dismembered body flitted through my mind. His lips tightened; was he seeing it too?

"Grunts don't have the same healing ability as the higher-level shade," he said evenly. "I guess if he'd been given enough time between injury …" He trailed off and averted his gaze.

Yeah, he was seeing it too. Recalling what his hands had done. Hard to heal when you were being dismembered. The words were on the tip of my tongue, but I bit them back. No need for the others to know the extent of the mutilation the Reaper had inflicted. Rivers would have disposed of the body by now—a body that had once been a human. Thank goodness this particular specimen had been a loner. No family to speak of. Not in Midnight anyway.

"I don't think he could leave the host body," Rivers continued. "I think that once they're in they can only be removed by being killed or expelled."

Yeah, it was the obvious conclusion and made a twisted sense. There had to be a consequence for the shades, a price they had to pay to gain a host. But then that meant Drayton was stuck with Xavier unless I could find a way to get him out. Expelling him hadn't worked and killing him would kill Drayton. Damn, there had to be a way.

Bane put the stack of pancakes in front of Rivers. "Eat up and then we'll go over what we know." He sat back down in his seat. "It seems that our best bet is to remove the shadows, but in the event that we fail, we need to come up with a plan B."

Boot falls interrupted his train of thought and we all glanced at the door as Orin popped his head into the kitchen. His face was flushed, his eyes bright. He looked … aroused?

Bane stiffened. "Orin?"

Orin licked his lips. "Lilith is here."

No, that couldn't be right. She'd had her quota of sexual energy already. Shit, if she demanded more now, how would I siphon it? I could barely contain the divine energy coursing through my veins. I shot Bane a panicked glance, but he was busy grinding his teeth into oblivion.

"She wants us all in the lounge. Now," Orin said.

All of us?

Bane pushed back his chair. "She has no right to be here. Not now. And she has no right to make demands." He glared at Ryker and me. "Stay here," he ordered before following Orin out of the room.

Ryker, Rivers, and I exchanged glances and then Ryker arched an enquiring brow.

I scraped my chair back. "Fuck it. Let's go see what the bitch wants."

We entered the lounge a minute or so after Bane, but it looked like he was already neck-deep in an argument with Lilith. The succubus, who was usually calm and collected, looked decidedly shaken. Her usually silken, groomed hair was ruffled and out of place, and her lips were bare of the crimson lipstick she usually sported. In fact, she looked very much as if she'd thrown on her clothes and run all the way over here.

Bane was standing by the hearth as usual, his arms crossed defensively across his chest. He didn't look over as we entered, but Lilith did. Her tense face relaxed a fraction.

"Please, come in and shut the door," she said softly. "In fact, lock it if you can."

"What the fuck is this about?" Bane said.

"I'll tell you now that everyone is here. Please, just be patient."

Ryker slid the door shut behind us and turned the key in the lock.

Lilith walked over to the drinks tray, poured a generous measure of whisky in a glass, and gulped it down. She blew out a breath and then turned to face the room.

"Lilith." Bane's tone was a warning. "You're trying my patience. I'm going to ask you one more time, and if I don't like your response, I *will* hurt you. Why. Are. You. Here?"

She smoothed her hair away from her face. "Ambrosius brought me."

"Ambrosius?" I took a step toward her. "What do you mean?"

She smiled at me. "He's a friend of yours, and for the last two weeks he's been harassing me, except I didn't know who he was. I couldn't see or hear him. But he made his presence known by banging and moving stuff. I thought I was being haunted. But a few hours ago, I finally heard his voice. He told me his name, and I knew it was time."

"Time for what?" Bane snapped.

She looked at him. "To release you from our contract."

Bane inhaled sharply, and an expression of longing flitted across his harsh face, and then his eyes hardened. "Is this some kind of joke?"

"No. It isn't," Lilith said. "A long time ago, you asked me to enter into this contract with you. You told me it was to facilitate an agreement between the White Wings and the Black Wings. You told me that the White Wings would never negotiate a stand-down with the Black Wings if you were around. So, you asked me to help you hide. You told me the contract would be over when Ambrosius came to call. I had no idea who Ambrosius was, and you didn't enlighten me."

What was she talking about? Knowledge pricked the back of my mind. I looked at Bane, but his face had drained of color, and he was shaking his head.

Lilith took a step toward him, her hand out as if to console him, but he jerked back. She caught her lip between her teeth. "Ambrosius explains it better." She ran a hand over her face. "Ambrosius, are you there?"

"I'm here." His voice was weak but audible.

My heart climbed up into my throat. He'd been gone for what felt like forever, and now he was back. I could hear him, and it felt like a missing piece of me had been restored.

It had been too long since we'd talked, but I was about to remedy that. "What's going on? Why did you bring Lilith here?"

"It's good to see you, Serenity," he said. "I'll answer all your questions now that I can. When you severed the connection between Merlin's body and me, I finally remembered everything." His voice was louder now, closer, as if he were standing next to me.

"A long time ago, Merlin drew the divine power out of the five weapons created by the White Wings. He cast a powerful spell to send it into the aether to hide there until a time when it was needed. Then it would find a home in a cambion soul. He knew that the veil would fall. He'd known that the world would need this power someday for a greater good, that humans and winged would need to work together. Before he left to try and seal the cracks in the veil, to buy us more time, he crafted the daggers and he left part of his soul behind with some of his memories."

"You. He left you."

"Yes. He linked the daggers to the weapon, so they could only be wielded by the chosen cambion. But he didn't do this alone. He collaborated with his friend, his confidant, Lucifer."

Lucifer … a chill trickled through my veins.

"Lucifer was afraid that the knowledge he had may fall into the wrong hands, that if the winged did manage to capture him, they may find a way of searching his mind and discover what Merlin had done with the power held inside the weapons. He couldn't risk them finding out and somehow foiling the plan. And so, he decided to hide his memories, even from himself."

"To kill two birds with one stone," Lilith said. "Hide the weapon and promote a truce between the winged."

"No, this is bullshit," Bane said.

I looked from Lilith's pale face to Bane's even paler one. And the penny dropped. Hard. My stomach clenched and panic bloomed like a mini supernova in my chest.

"I didn't know about the veil or the daggers," Lilith said to Bane. "You never told me. I guess you didn't trust me enough. You told me half the story and we cast a powerful glamour, one that you could only sustain if I siphoned your power every few months. Because if I didn't, the glamour would crack and your true form would be revealed."

"No." Bane's body was vibrating with denial.

It was Ambrosius who replied. "Lucifer, my friend. It's time to wake up. Only you can bring the winged forces together to fight this threat. We need you now. Bane has served his purpose, but from this point on, the winged need their general."

He'd said it, said what I'd just been thinking, and there was no taking it back now. Breath exploded from my lungs.

Bane was Lucifer.

I locked gazes with him, and he shook his head, but the fire had bled out of his eyes. He knew it. He knew it was true. Deep down, he knew …

Lilith's focus was on me now. "I'm sorry, Serenity. I tried to warn you not to get too attached. I urged you to lean on your cambion nature to soften the blow. The man you fell in love with is a facade, a fabrication. If we are to move forward and overcome this threat, then you must let him go."

Bane was no fabrication. He was a living, breathing neph with memories and emotions, and yes, I loved him. I fucking loved him, and no one was taking him away from me.

"No." I walked up to Bane and stood in front of him as if my body could act as a shield to prevent whatever she intended to do. "I won't let you do it."

Bane's hands closed over my shoulders, his familiar warmth seeping into my skin. "I'm not going anywhere."

Lilith's smile was filled with sympathy. "You don't have a choice. Without your power being siphoned, your glamour will crack, and once it does, you will be back in your real body. You *will* be Lucifer again with all your memories restored. Bane will be nothing but a dream."

A vise closed around my chest. "No. There has to be a way to stop it. We need Bane, not Lucifer." I looked to Ryker, Rivers, and Orin for backup, but they looked stunned, confused, and shaken.

Ryker was the first to respond. "Bane isn't a dream. He's my friend. I have no idea what this Lucifer is like, and I'm not interested in finding out."

Rivers crossed his arms. "Find a way to stop it." His gaze was icy and directed at Lilith.

Orin tucked his chin in, lips pressed tightly together as if holding back a tide of words.

I couldn't siphon Bane's power, I was too filled with my own, but Lilith could if she wanted. "You have to siphon the excess," I demanded.

That sad smile again. "No. I made a deal, and I will not break it. Lucifer told me that he may resist. He made me vow to bring him back. I am here to honor that vow."

Dammit. I wanted to hit her.

Bane's grip on my shoulders tightened. "Give us the room. Now."

The guys filed out of the room, but Lilith lingered a moment by the door. "I'm sorry. I really am."

"The greater good," Ambrosius's voice whispered in my ear.

I squeezed my eyes shut, pushing down the tears. "Just go."

He withdrew, the door to the lounge closed, and I was alone with Bane. He turned me to face him and claimed my mouth. It was a desperate, aching kiss, with the bittersweet taste of goodbye.

"No." I pulled away. "No ..."

He cupped my face. "I have to." His throat bobbed. "For as long as I can remember I've felt uncomfortable in this skin, as if there was something missing, and now I know why. My anger, my discontent ... I think they were all a symptom of this glamour. It makes sense now. If not for you, I wouldn't even be hesitating right now, because Lilith is right. As Lucifer, I can bring the winged together. Lucifer can achieve what Bane cannot. The White Wings will allow him entrance to Dawn. He may be able to get through to them. Bane ... Right now, Bane is only good enough for loving you."

Oh, God. Please. I clasped his jaw. "Isn't that enough?"

His gaze, which was usually as hard as flint, softened. "Serenity ..."

"You won't be Bane anymore." I stroked his chest with the palm of my hand. "This ... all this will be gone."

He grabbed my hand and pressed it to his breast bone. "But this heart that loves you will remain the same." He inhaled me, pressing his nose to my brow. "And this scent is woven into my mind. I won't. I can't forget it."

But he didn't get it. He didn't understand that Bane would be discarded. The man I loved would be ripped to shreds. "Don't leave me. Please." My eyes burned and the tears slid free. "I need you. I love you."

He exhaled through his nose and closed his eyes for a long beat, and then he dropped his forehead to mine. "Fuck, Harker. If I could stay … If the world wasn't going to shit right now … I have to do this. But I have to believe that I'll find you again, because, Harker, you're etched onto my fucking heart."

The sob trapped in my throat escaped, and I buried my head in his chest, my hands fisting his T-shirt. His arms wrapped around me, holding me so tight it felt as if he would never let go, which was good, because this was where I wanted to be.

He pulled back and smoothed my hair away from my face. His eyes were misty and his voice hoarse. "You won't be alone when I'm gone. Ryker, Orin, and Rivers are here for you. They care about you. They love you, Harker. You just need to allow them in." He stroked my face, his eyes scanning my features as if committing them to memory. "Promise me you'll accept who and what you are. Promise me you will let them love you."

I swallowed the lump in my throat and nodded through my tears. My chest ached, my heart ached. This couldn't be happening, but it was.

"I don't know how focused Lucifer will be on the MPD, so I need you to step into my shoes. You're a natural leader, Harker." His lips quirked in a wry smile. "One of the reasons we were always knocking heads. The MPD will need direction once I'm gone.

We need to finish what we started. Promise me."

I nodded, my throat too tight to speak.

Bane pressed a hard kiss to my forehead and then released me and walked to the door.

He slid it open. "Let's get this over with. What do we have to do?"

"Not us," Lilith said. "Serenity."

I held Bane's hand as he lay on his bed. I'd never seen the man anything but confident before, but in that moment, he was shrouded in doubt and nervousness. Lilith placed a hand on my shoulder, and the urge to slap it away was almost too much, but this wasn't her fault. She was doing what Lucifer had made her vow to do. My head was fuzzy from crying and everything felt numb. It was up to me to force the glamour apart. Up to me to channel my cambion power into him.

"Not the divine power," Lilith reminded me. "He is a Black Wing and that could hurt him."

"I got it, okay." My hands trembled as I laid them on his chest, just over his heart. That heartbeat that I'd teased into a gallop on more than one occasion jumped once beneath my palm.

Bane nodded and closed his eyes.

"Do it," Lilith said.

I shook my head. "I can't."

"Harker, you have to," Bane said gruffly.

"Serenity." My name on her lips was saturated

with compassion.

Eyes burning, throat tight, I focused on his face, his beautiful feral features. "Goodbye, Bane." The words were thick with emotion.

Bane squeezed my hand, and with a deep breath, I channeled my cambion power into him. He grit his teeth, perspiration beading his forehead.

"More," Lilith ordered.

With a strangled sob, I expelled more power. The relief was immense as the divine power filled the gaps that my own power left. But it was killing Bane. I was killing him. No. I couldn't do this. I couldn't. I made to pull my hand away and he opened his eyes. Shining bright violet orbs gazed up at me.

"Serenity …" My name was a caress on his lips. "I wish I could …" And then he exploded into a thousand fragments of light.

A scream lodged in my throat. Lilith grabbed me and pulled me back. We hit the floor by the bed as the energy—Bane's energy—circled like a mini tornado. The air currents whipped my hair into my face, and the room was lit up by a rainbow hue of light. And then it stopped as if someone had flipped a switch.

Lilith rose to her feet and held out her hand to me. She hauled me up and together we moved toward the bed.

My knees trembled, my pulse raced. Bane was gone. In his place lay an ebony-haired, aquiline-nosed, beautiful man. His body was huge, but whereas Bane had been bulky muscle, this guy had an athletic build. Whereas Bane's face had been ferocious and feral, this dude was perfectly proportioned. This was Lucifer, the Black Wing who had taken Bane from me.

I turned away. "How long before he wakes up?" My voice was flat.

"I don't know. Would you like to stay with him until he wakes?" Her tone was soft, hesitant.

"No. I don't know who that man on the bed is. The man I loved is gone."

I walked out of the room, a tsunami brewing in my chest, and bumped into Rivers's taut chest. His hands came out to steady me.

"Serenity?"

I nodded. "It's done. I just … I can't be with him when he wakes up. I can't …"

Rivers released me, his back straightening. "Then I'll do it for you."

My throat closed up with emotion, and on impulse I wrapped my arms around his waist and pressed the side of my head to his chest. His heartbeat picked up and then resumed a steady, strong beat. And after a moment, his arms wrapped around me, and he squeezed me back.

"It will be okay, Serenity," he said. "We'll make it okay."

I pulled back, the throb in my temples, the need to scream and cry building, ready to explode. "I have to go."

I walked to the end of the corridor, and then I ran.

He would never wrap me in his arms and take me for

a moonlit flight. We'd never share our favorite chocolate biscuits again. I'd never hold him and breathe in his scent, and I'd never hear him say my name, rough and irritated but indulgent at the same time.

We never even got to have that date. When people talked about a broken heart, I'd always believed it was metaphorical, but it wasn't. It really wasn't, because mine was breaking now, and it bloody hurt.

My pillow was soaked with tears, my eyes swollen shut, and I didn't even hear them enter my bedroom. It was their distinctive scents that tipped me off, that and the dip of the bed as they climbed on. Orin was cinnamon and sugar, reminding me of the rolls he loved to bake. My throat tightened with nostalgia. Ryker was a summer breeze that filled me with yearning for the sunlight. They snuggled up on either side of me, cocooning me in my grief. Ryker pulled me against his chest and pressed kisses to my brow. He smoothed back my hair, forcing me to look up at him through swollen, slitted eyelids. I was snotty and gross. A tissue appeared in front of my face, held by Orin. Ryker plucked it from his fingers and gently wiped my face clean. Orin's arm wrapped around my waist and he tucked in his chin to press his face against the nape of my neck. Our legs tangled, and a sigh, part sob, part laugh, rattled my chest. They were here, just like Bane had said they'd be.

"Drayton's gone and now Bane too." I clutched at Ryker's shirt with one hand and fumbled for Orin's hand with the other. "I can't lose you too. Promise me you won't leave. Promise."

In that moment, I didn't care how desperate or weak I sounded. In that moment, my heart was an open, weeping wound that only they could heal.

"I'm not going anywhere," Ryker said, his gaze crystalline-clear and determined.

"Me either." Orin's grip on me tightened. "I swear it, Serenity. You'll never lose me."

"We're here," Ryker added.

Orin shouldn't be making these promises. He shouldn't be pledging himself to me, he had Cassie, but the thought was fleeting, buried under my need for him—his warmth, his compassion, his arms like foundations holding me up. And Ryker, the man who knew my heart. They held me together when the temptation to fall apart was at its worst.

My breaking heart swelled with a new sensation, not grief, not loss, but love—overwhelming and breathtaking. And with it came another sensation, sharp and greedy—mine, it said. They were mine.

The door opened with a snick.

"Orin?" Cassie's voice trembled.

My body tensed and my grip on Orin's fingers tightened reflexively.

He squeezed my hand. "Not now, Cassie. Not now."

"But—"

"We'll talk later," Orin said.

The door closed. Ryker pulled the throw over us. "Sleep, babe. We're here."

I'd lost Drayton, and I'd lost Bane, but I'd be damned if I'd lose Rivers, Orin, and Ryker. We were a team, and it was my job to keep us together.

Still hope for Drayton, my daimon whispered. *Still hope for Bane*. Her optimism was soothing, and my muscles slowly unknotted. I closed my eyes and allowed exhaustion to claim me.

I awoke to lamplight and warmth. I must have turned over in my sleep because now it was Orin whose chest I was lying on and Ryker who was hugging my back.

"Serenity. Serenity, can you hear me?"

"Ambrosius?" I carefully extricated myself from Orin and Ryker and sat up. "Why can't I see you? Are you a ghost?"

"No. Not a ghost. I'm … something else. But you *can* see me if you use your aether-sight."

Shit, of course. I switched sight and the world went gray. "Where are you?"

"Right in front of you."

There was no one there. "I can't see you."

"You need to shift gears, cycle through the layers of the aether."

"What are you talking about? What layers?"

He sighed. "Are you telling me you've been stuck on one channel?"

"I didn't realize there was more than one, and since when are you such an expert?"

"I don't know. Knowledge flooded me when you severed the cord binding me to Merlin's body. I just know things. Try peeling back a layer."

"And how do I do that?"

"It's like looking deeper."

Okay. It was worth a shot. I focused on one spot and pressed with my mind—deeper, further. The gray bled into blue and a figure appeared—tall and broad with a neatly clipped beard. He didn't look like the massive monolith Merlin who'd stepped out from beyond the veil. He looked young, probably mid-twenties.

This had been the voice inside my head? A tired smile tugged at my lips. "Hello, Ambrosius."

He returned my smile, but his gaze was concerned. "I'm sorry if my knowledge brought you pain. I never meant to hurt you in any way, Serenity. During our time together, I have grown to care deeply for you."

"It's not your fault. These events were set into motion over a century ago. You were just as much a pawn as me."

He sighed and walked closer to the bed. "But you aren't alone." He looked from Ryker to Orin. "You will never be alone. And that is good, because the road ahead will be hard. You are our sole weapon against the shades, and you will need to remain stoic and strong."

"That's the last thing I feel right now."

"Take this moment to grieve, but then you must pick yourself back up and get back in the fight, because without you, we are all defenseless."

He was right, and I hated it. With Bane at the helm, things hadn't seemed so bad, but now he was gone … Who would lead us? Not Lucifer. He was a Black Wing. He was one of the winged, not a neph. Who'd tell me that I was being difficult, or unreasonable, or just plain pigheaded? I closed my eyes. I'd have to do it for myself. I'd have to keep my promise and lead.

"There's something else you should know," Ambrosius said. "The humans here are being fed on."

I was instantly alert. "What? By who?"

"By the dead. There are souls here. Ghouls who have attached themselves to the humans and are feeding off their life force and their energy. If they are not stopped, then the humans could die."

Something niggled at the back of my brain. Something someone had recently said to me … Rivers! He'd said something about the humans being weakened so it was easy for the shades to take over their conscious minds. Oh, God. All the sick humans in the hospital were being fed off psychically. Were the ghouls deliberately working with the shades or was it just a happy coincidence for the shades? It didn't matter, because it was time to put a stop to it.

I quickly filled Ambrosius in. "Marika is working on figuring out a way to separate the humans from their shadows, to stop the shades from accessing the humans. But even if she finds a way to do that, we still need to stop the ghouls from killing the humans."

His gaze sharpened. "You cannot strip a human of its shadow. The shadow is bound to the human soul."

"But the Sanguinata don't have shadows, so there must be a way."

"The Sanguinata are neph, and nephs are different. For nephs, the shadow is a useless appendage, like the human appendix. We don't *need* it. The Sanguinata must have evolved to shed theirs naturally. But a human without a shadow will die just as surely as if you'd cut his throat."

Oh, fuck. "Then what do we do?"

"The shades were cast out of this world by God."

"They were?"

Ambrosius nodded. "Yes. Merlin knew this from his vision of the future. There will be places on this plane where they cannot walk. Hallowed ground. We must focus on finding hallowed ground, and once we do, we must move as many humans as we can, as many as will listen, to safety. Then we can focus on ridding Midnight of the ghouls."

It was a solid plan, and purpose washed away the lethargy infusing my limbs. Bane would have expected us to carry on and get this shit sorted, and I knew just how to do it. The clock told me it was six in the morning.

I gently shook Ryker's shoulder. "It's time to wake up, babe. It's time to summon the Piper."

After a quick breakfast consisting mainly of coffee, the guys and I split up to take care of various tasks. Ryker had taken on the responsibility of updating the Black Wings in the east wing about Lucifer's return—another fail in the whole *keeping them in the loop* thing. Orin had excused himself to speak with Cassie—a fail on my part for not kicking him when she'd come looking for him. Guilt was a shroud that was becoming all too familiar; it sat snug on my shoulders as I was headed to the west wing to update Marika on what Ambrosius had told me.

Marika opened her door clutching a book. She looked taller. I glanced down, and the reason why stared back at me in the form of bright red stilettos. She followed my gaze down to her feet and then laughed.

"Thought I'd break them in for after all this is over. I am so going dancing." She kicked them off and ushered me in.

She wasn't alone. A guy lounged on the bed with another book and two females sat opposite each other in high-backed chairs by the window. They were all reading or making notes, their faces drawn and pale. Huge mugs of steaming coffee sat on the window sill, probably to combat their obvious fatigue. Shit, they must be feeling the effects of the ghouls. How many were in the room with us now?

Marika yawned.

Had she slept at all? Not that it would help if she was being fed off. "It's barely eight in the morning. Did you get some sleep?"

"Yeah, we just hit the books again about an hour ago. Wanted to get to it and find a solution. I guess you want an update on the shadow stripping thing?" Marika held up her book. "We managed to grab the books we needed, but so far, no joy." She held up a finger. "But I have hope."

I winced. "I don't."

Her brows shot up, and I filled her in on what Ambrosius had told me.

"Damn." She shut her book with a snap. "Guys, cool it. We have confirmation that it can't be done. Humans can't be stripped of shadows."

A series of groans filled the room.

"But nephs can," Ambrosius said.

I started, hand going to my chest. "Dammit, Ambrosius. Some warning, please."

"I thought you could see me."

"I don't wander around in aether-sight. It gives me a headache."

"Sorry." He sounded contrite and my irritation melted. "I will announce my presence in the future."

"Thanks."

Marika was silent, her mouth parted in awe.

"Ambrosius? Merlin's soul-piece, Ambrosius?"

"I like to think of myself as an independent entity," Ambrosius said stiffly.

Marika bit back a smile. "I'm sorry. It's just, Order of Merlin and all that."

"Yes. Merlin-bloods." There was a smile in his voice.

"Wait? What?" Marika scanned the air.

"You all have his blood in your veins," Ambrosius replied. "Did you not know this?"

"Um, no." Behind her, the other Order members sat up straighter, intrigued.

"All arcane manipulators can be traced back to Merlin. He was a … prolific procreator, and being cambion meant his appetites were voracious."

This was so weird. He was talking about himself and yet not.

"I can sense his power in this room," he continued. "In all of you. Asher knows this, of course. It is why he used the Order to help the shades break free. But you … you are different."

"Who?" Marika glanced about.

"You. Marika. That is your name, isn't it?"

Marika looked at me. "How am I different?"

I shrugged, and there was a long beat of silence.

"I do not know," Ambrosius said finally.

Marika clapped her hands together. "Okay, well, then let's not stress about it, shall we. We need to get back to work on the shadow problem. Find a solution for the nephs."

"The solution is standing in front of you," Ambrosius said. "Serenity's dagger can make the cut for the nephs and sever them from their shadows."

Marika threw up her hands. "Now where the heck were you a day ago?" She shook her head. "All this bloody reading for nothing," she muttered.

I tucked in my chin. She didn't know about Lilith's arrival, or Bane or Lucifer. It was stuff they needed to know, but the words were like ashes on my tongue. As if picking up on my thoughts, Ambrosius began to speak. He told them about his trip, about Lilith and Bane and what he really was. When he was done, the room was filled with an awkward silence.

Marika was the first to break it. "I'm sorry about Bane, Harker. He was a great guy, a little abrasive but cool."

Something twisted in my chest, stealing my breath. For a moment, my hard-woman facade cracked and my emotions rose to the surface. I grabbed at them, pushing them back down.

Marika cleared her throat. "Well. It seems we have a plan, then. We use the daggers to liberate the nephs and cut off the shades' supply of neph hosts. But we still need to do something about the humans."

"I have a plan for that. Ambrosius suggested finding hallowed ground. Somewhere where the shades may not be able to roam? Maybe we can ward another building?"

"No." Marika shook her head. "The spell that is holding the wards up channels arcane power through us. We've been struggling to maintain them as it is."

"What about Respite?" the guy on the bed said.

Marika's brows shot up, and she pursed her lips. "Possibly."

"The cemetery? How can that help us?"

"It may not," Marika said. "But rumor has it

99

that the area is supernaturally guarded by the souls that live there. Maybe it could be a safe zone? We won't know until we ask."

Another thought occurred to me. What if the ghouls couldn't get into Respite either? Doris would know. "Leave it with me. I'll speak to the soul who kinda runs the place. If this works, then we can move the fatigued humans at the hospital first. They're being fed on psychically by ghouls. It's weakening them and making them easy prey for shades."

Marika's eyes widened and she looked around the room at her exhausted posse. "The ghouls are feeding off humans?"

I winced. "Yeah. Sorry, did I not mention that?" Man, my brain was fried.

She licked her lips nervously. "Are there any here now?"

I switched to aether-sight and scanned the room, then delved deeper. Ambrosius appeared by my side and then something flickered in the periphery of my vision—a blue, wispy, partial figure floating above the guy on the bed. The guy yawned as if on cue.

"One."

She rubbed her temples. "I guess the wards around this place must be deterring the shades, otherwise we'd all be goners. It also explains why maintaining the wards has been so hard. With the ghouls draining us psychically, there is no way we'd be able to maintain another set of wards. We need to do something more, though, because I'm not hiding behind these walls in fear of becoming infected, and I'm not hiding out in the cemetery either. We need to get rid of the ghouls."

I smiled mirthlessly. "And we will. We just need to summon death."

She blinked in surprise but didn't question me. "Just tell us what you need us to do."

Leaving Ambrosius with Marika, I went in search of Oleander. He was probably in the kitchen; it was supper time, and he'd made it his prime objective to feed everyone, but his skills would be better served helping Marika with our Piper summoning. If Marika couldn't find anything in her books, then we'd have to check out our library, and then the Black Wings' library at the mansion. Abigor or Abbadon could fly the ancient over to the cliff house to go through their tomes if need be. The more eyes and brains on the problem, the more likely we were to solve it.

I rounded the corner leading to the steps down to the kitchen and stopped short at the sight of Cassie. She froze for a fraction of a second and a series of emotions flitted across her face—surprise, anger, and… Was that resignation?

"I was actually coming to find you," she said.

My stomach clenched. "If this is about Orin being in my room last night, then I'm sorry. He shouldn't have been there. I was upset. I wasn't thinking. I should have made him leave." But I hadn't wanted to, and guilt was a real, writhing thing in my chest. There was no excuse. None. And she had every reason to be pissed at me.

She closed her eyes briefly, her smile tight.

"It's not up to you to make him *do* anything, Harker. That's the whole fucking point." She shook her head. "I was coming to tell you that I'm done. Orin and I are done. It's not working, it hasn't been for some time, but I thought when I came back that things could be different, but I see I was too late." She paused a moment as if gathering the words. "While I was gone, he fell in love with you."

The words were like a punch to my chest. My ears heated and my eyes grew hot. "It's not like that. We're friends. He cares about me."

My words were hollow to my ears because deep down I didn't believe them. It was hard to make excuses when someone was so blunt with the truth. It was difficult to hide from what you were picking up on when someone threw it in your face.

"You know it, Harker. You've just been running from it, and I appreciate that. I do. But I'm not the kind of chick that holds onto someone that would rather be elsewhere. It won't make him love me again."

"Orin chose you. He chose to be with you."

She flinched. "Yeah? But he was with you last night." She sighed. "I get it. He feels bad for what I went through, and he wants to be the good guy by sticking it out and picking up the pieces. And I thought it would be enough, that with a little time, together we'd get back to the place we'd been." She shrugged. "But I deserve better. I deserve loyalty."

Whoa, wait a minute. "*You're* the one who went off with Killion all the time, even *before* you were infected with the shade. So, if anything, it's Orin who deserves better."

Her mouth twisted. "And the truth comes out. I knew the softly, softly nice approach was an act. And FYI, we were in an open relationship."

"Open for you. But Orin wasn't fucking anyone else."

Her mouth pursed like she'd sucked on a lemon. "No, he wasn't. But he is now, maybe not actually fucking, but wishing he could. Sleeping in the same bed, holding you, all that crap, it's cheating just the same as if he stuck his cock in you."

My face burned because she was right. There was no excuse, and I'd allowed him to be close to me knowing he was back with her.

"You're right. I'm sorry. I should have put more of a distance between us. I should have made him leave last night."

She blew out a sharp breath. "Fuck it. As much as it would feel good to push all the blame onto you, I can't. He tried to tell me. He tried a couple of times, and I shut him down. I brought up my trauma and used guilt to force him to keep his mouth shut. I knew he'd stay, that he'd sacrifice what he really wanted. But it doesn't feel good. Not anymore. I can't do it anymore, and so it's over."

"For what it's worth, he really did love you. You have no idea what it did to him when you went off with Killion."

Her eyes hardened to ice chips. "And what do you think it will do to him to see you with Rivers or Ryker? You think he'll be able to handle being one of many?" Her lip curled. "If he couldn't cope with me seeing Killion, then how the heck do you think he'll cope with you 'snuggling' with Ryker or fucking

Rivers."

It was like she'd punched me in the gut. "Rivers and I haven't—"

"Not yet, but you will. I see the way he looks at you. That icy intensity he reserves for his tech projects. Things he wants to take apart and put back together again. He has impeccable control but it's not infinite, and he's always close to losing it around you." She chuckled mirthlessly. "I wonder what it will be like to fuck the ice king?"

Rivers's hands on my skin, his mouth crushing mine as he ground me into the wall. If there was ice there, then it had been on fire. Shit. I averted my gaze.

"Orin won't be able to cope." The edge had dropped from her tone. "He'll try to be the man you need. He'll try to share you, but each time you're with one of the others, you'll take a piece of him."

Was she right? Is that what being with me would do to him? Orin. Sweet, kind Orin. The thought of hurting him, of bringing him any kind of pain, made my insides twist.

"Up until now, Orin and I have been friends, but … if he wants to be more, then I won't turn him away."

Bane's words echoed in my ear. *Promise me you'll accept who and what you are. Promise me you will let them love you.* I'd been afraid at first. Afraid to let my guard down and feel, but the guys each reached out to me in different ways. I found a new piece of myself with each of them, and together they made me feel safe enough to accept myself and finally be whole.

I met Cassie's gaze steadily. "I'm a cambion, and when we love, we love with every fiber of our being, and I love the guys. I love them, and if they want me, then I'm not going to turn my back on what we could have."

Finally, my daimon sighed. The knot in my stomach, the one that had been there forever, or so it seemed, loosened.

Cassie gave me a hard smile. "You think it's going to be easy. You think your pretty face and body will be enough for them? They may be nephs, but they're still guys, and one thing I've learned about guys is that all they want is to be the alpha, and when it comes to women, they all want to possess her. So, yeah. Good luck with that." Cassie took a deep breath and exhaled. "Okay. Now we have that out of the way. What's the plan? Orin said you'd taken over the reins. What can I do to help?"

She was done, but she was wrong. However, there was no point arguing with her when she was hurting. There was no point arguing full stop. There was too much at stake to worry about love right now. I'd made Bane a promise—to be okay—and I would. But first I needed to make sure the MPD made good on our vow to protect the humans of this district, and Cassie was a fucking awesome MPD officer. We needed her, and from the looks of it, she was ready to put personal crap on hold to be there.

I nodded curtly. "Walk with me, and I'll fill you in."

Oleander had been safely dispatched to help Marika, the Black Wings were on standby to take him to the cliff house if needed, and Ava and Cassie were waiting on my call once I had confirmation that Respite was hallowed. Rivers was still with Bane, and Ryker had said he'd drive me, but it had been Orin who'd climbed into the driver's seat of the van. He hadn't spoken, just started the engine and hit the gas.

We were on the main road before I broke the silence. "Where's Ryker?"

"I told him I'd drive you," Orin said.

"Why?"

He was tight-lipped and silent for a long beat. "What did Cassie say to you?"

God, what hadn't she said? "Just that you guys weren't together anymore."

"And?"

I threw up my hands. "Does it matter? She was upset. She said some things. I said some things. It's over."

"Did she tell you why it's over?"

Oh … He wanted to know if I knew how he felt. My neck heated. "She said you were in love with me."

The van swerved to the curb, and he hit the brakes. He sat there, chest heaving, hands gripping the wheel so tight I thought he would take the whole thing off.

"Orin?"

"I'm sorry," he said. "I lied to you when I said you and I were just friends. I shouldn't have done that."

He felt guilty? He had no idea. A choked laugh

escaped my lips, and he turned his head to look at me, his beautiful face knitted in a frown.

"You think this is funny?" he asked softly, almost as if he couldn't believe it.

"No, not funny, just … ironic. If anyone has anything to feel guilty about, it's me. I lied when I said I wanted things to work with you and Cassie. I lied when I told myself you should be with her and not me. And even though I knew it was wrong, I thought about you anyway, in ways that a friend shouldn't." I swallowed hard. "I thought about you touching me … kissing me … wanting me."

His breath exploded from his lips. "You want me?"

His face, the incredulous fucking look on his face. Did he have no clue? I needed to make him understand, but simple words wouldn't do. Now that Cassie and he were officially over and the guilty tangle inside me was gone, it seemed natural to unbuckle my seat belt and climb over to straddle him.

His hands settled lightly on my hips, almost as if he was afraid that if he touched me too firmly I'd shatter.

I cupped his face and looked into his eyes. "I want you, Orin. Not just with my body, but with my heart too." I kissed his forehead softly and then his eyelids. "Nothing chases away the nightmares like your arms around me. Nothing makes me feel more at home than the smell of your fucking scones. You make me feel safe. You make me feel like I've come home." I kissed him feather-light, just a brush of my lips, because if I kissed him, really kissed him right now, then I'd be lost.

His fingers tightened a fraction on my hips, sending a lance of yearning through me. There was no longer any hunger, not anymore. But I felt it anyway. It was a hunger for him, a desire that stemmed from my heart, not the cavern of emptiness that required power to fulfill it. Right now, I wanted Orin, and not his power.

I made to pull away, but he tilted his chin and captured my mouth with his, parting my lips and sweeping his tongue into my mouth. It was smooth and fucking sexy as hell. For a moment my resolve cracked and my body melted into him. My crotch throbbed against his hardness and my abdomen pressed to his chest as he played my mouth with his lips, filling me with the sweet, sugary taste of butterscotch. My head reeled with sensation and scent, and my hands ached to feel his skin against my palms. But letting go was not an option right now. Bane had entrusted me with the responsibility of getting rid of the shades. I needed to focus.

I pulled away from Orin, eliciting an uncharacteristic growl that made my core throb and almost melted my resolve.

I licked my lips. "When this is over …"

He ran his thumb across my bottom lip, and it took everything I had not to take it in my mouth.

"When this is over," he echoed.

We resumed our journey, what could be between us on hold, for now.

Doris greeted us with suspicious eyes. "What do you

want now?" She looked Orin up and down. "No Bane today?"

I didn't have it in me to go into detail, and just the mention of his name hurt my heart. "Doris, we need your help. You may have sensed changes outside of Respite. It's to do with those changes."

She snorted in disgust. "If you mean the lost souls floating around, then yes." She pulled a packet of cigarettes from her pocket and sparked up. "They hover from time to time, drawn to this place. But they never stay long."

"Can they get in?" Orin asked.

"No. This is *our* place—a place for the murdered residents of Midnight. Those souls have no clue what it is to truly die. They hold on to life, eager for it, leeching from the living instead of finding their own special peace."

"So, there's some kind of barrier preventing them from getting onto the grounds."

Doris cocked her head. "Why all the questions? What is it you want?"

"We have a problem, and I need you to help fix it."

She took a puff of her nicotine stick. "I'm listening."

I told her about the shades, the ghouls, and the humans. "Is this hallowed ground? Would the shades be able to get into the cemetery?"

Her eyes were now slits. "You want to bring the living onto our land? Living humans wandering around Respite? Pitching tents and making campfires? Is this some kind of joke?"

"So it *is* hallowed," Orin said.

She shot him an irritated look. "Yes. This is protected ground. Humans and neph can enter, but anything that is an abomination, like the scourge or The Breed, cannot, and these shades ... We've seen them hovering at the gates. We wondered what they were, and now we know. They are abominations, and they won't be able to enter here."

My heart was thudding real fast. This was it. This was our solution, temporary, but it was something. We just needed her okay. "Doris, please ..."

She looked off into the distance.

We needed to give her something. Anything. "If you do this for us, we'll owe you. Big time." It was weak, but it was all I had—a big, fat IOU.

She blinked, her gaze becoming super-focused. "*You* will owe me. Personally. And I *will* collect." She took a final drag on her cigarette and flicked it into oblivion. "Bring your humans. We will keep them safe as long as you need us to."

I sagged in relief. "Thank you."

Her ruby red lips curved in a sly smile. "Oh, don't thank me just yet, Harker. You have no idea what I'll want in return."

A shiver slipped up my spine, but I suppressed it. "I pay my debts, Doris. Always."

She vanished back into the mausoleum, and Orin and I walked out the arch toward the van.

"Let's get back to the mansion," Orin said. "At least we have one bit of good news now."

I reached for my phone, intent on calling Ava, but a movement at the periphery of my vision had me pausing, and then a figure stepped out of the shadows.

Orin pulled me back, placing my body between him and the newcomer, between me and Drayton. Damn, I really needed to stop thinking of him as that. Xavier, his name was Xavier.

Orin's body was a tense mass ready to attack, but Xavier didn't make a move. Instead, he held up his hands, and took a step back. He looked … confused.

I gripped Orin's bicep and gave it a reassuring squeeze. "What are you doing here, Xavier?"

He shook his head. "I … I'm not sure." He blinked rapidly and then backed up another step. "So, this is the dead zone where no shade may pass?" He smiled, and it was pretty obvious he was going for cocky, but the whole thing was slightly off. He was covering.

Orin must have sensed it too because his muscles relaxed beneath my fingers, and he didn't stop me when I stepped around him.

"Why are you really here, Xavier?"

"Recon," he said. He was settling into the lie. "What are *you* doing here?"

I crossed my arms. "Oh, wait, are you really expecting me to tell you anything? You storm the district, you take over humans, and you try to kill Black Wings."

"Yes, I think you covered it all, aside from the fact that I also have your lover's body."

"Drayton and I were never lovers."

He smirked. "But you wanted to be. At least *he* did."

Orin took a menacing step toward Xavier. "Give me one good reason why I shouldn't pummel the fuck out of you."

Xavier swept a hand up and down his body. "You want to hurt your friend's casing, then go ahead."

He thought our hands were tied, but thanks to Rivers's interrogation, we had some fresh knowledge. "No. There's no point pummeling you. It's a waste of time, so is trying to expel you." I cocked my head. "But I can burn you to hell."

"And kill Drayton?" He arched a brow.

"He's dead anyway, because you're stuck in that body."

Xavier's smile faltered.

"Yeah, we know about that. Once a shade is in a host, it's stuck unless expelled or killed by me. There *is* no way to get you out without hurting him, and I know Drayton would rather die than be a prisoner in his own body."

Xavier's smug smile fell. "Wait a minute."

I strode toward him, power surging up through my veins, eyes pricking. It was time to set Drayton free. Time to let him have peace.

Xavier staggered back, his hand coming up to clutch his head. "Wait. Don't. Trying …"

Orin grabbed my elbow. "Fuck. Serenity, did you hear that?"

But I was already frozen to the spot, because although Xavier spoke with Drayton's voice, the inflection was different … until now. Until this moment. Those words hadn't been Xavier's, they'd been Drayton's.

"Drayton?"

Xavier straightened. "What? What did you

say?"

Once again, there was that look of confusion. He didn't know he'd spoken … just like he didn't know why he was here. A shocking revelation bloomed in my chest. Drayton was fighting back. Not sure how, but he was, and he'd just warned me to back off.

Orin caught my eye and shook his head slightly. Yeah, not the time to engage or let on that anything was amiss, but Xavier was still waiting for a response.

"I asked what you'd done with Abbadon. Why do you even need him?" It was the first thing that popped into my head, and a damned good question too.

"You really expect me to answer that?" Xavier asked.

"No. But can you at least tell us if he's alive?"

"Yes. He's alive."

I didn't know Xavier, but I knew Drayton's facial expressions, and this one was depicting shame. What the fuck did Xavier have to be ashamed about?

He stiffened. "I have to go." Then he turned and ran.

Orin and I stood staring at the spot where he'd just been. Orin was the first to break the silence. "Drayton's alive."

And he'd steered Xavier here, to the cemetery, but why? Dammit. If he was fighting, then there had to be a way to get rid of Xavier. We just needed to find it.

"We need to catch Xavier," Orin said. "If we can catch him and hold him, maybe we can figure this out."

"But if Drayton is fighting back on the sly then won't that tip Xavier off?"

Orin paced, agitated. "We have to do something. He's trapped."

I reached out and grabbed his arm. "Stop. There's nothing we can do right now. We have to focus on the task at hand. Drayton's smart, and if that was really him we heard, then he'll find a way to contact us again, and by that time we may have some answers as to how to help set him free."

My phone rang shrilly in my pocket. The caller ID flashed *Rivers*. I answered it as we climbed into the van. "Hey?"

"Harker, he's awake."

Orin drove us smoothly back toward the mansion. My hands trembled as I clutched the mobile to my ear, still reeling from the phone call with Rivers—short and sweet—while trying desperately to focus on what Ava was saying to me now.

"He's awake."

The words still echoed in my ear. I was on autopilot, speaking to Ava but only listening with half an ear. The rest of me was back at the mansion, walking up to Bane's bedroom door, heart in my mouth as I pushed it open. That other part of me squeezed Orin's fingers a little too tightly. He wrapped my hand in his, steering with the other. Drayton was alive and fighting and Bane had given himself up to allow Lucifer to rise. It seemed like fate was playing with me. Taking away with one hand and giving back with the other.

It was going to be okay. I could do this. Ava was silent on the other end of the line. What had I just said to her? Had she responded?

"Harker. Just tell me what you need me to do

and then leave it to me," Ava said.

This was usually Bane's domain. He was the delegator, not me. But he'd slipped the reins into my unwilling hands, and failure was not an option. Focus was essential right now. Deal with the call, and *then* stress about going back to the mansion. Ava and her unit were patrolling with the Protectorate. They'd been at it since five this morning and it was now mid-afternoon. Her shift was about to end, and I was dumping more work on her. Cassie was on her way to link up with the unit. I felt like a dick handing her more chores, but this wasn't something that could wait. We had the go-ahead, and we needed to move. Besides, she'd have Cassie to split the workload with—my way of assuaging the guilt.

I cleared my throat. "Liaise with Langley and work out a way to move the fatigued humans to the cemetery. Once we have them there, we can work on trying to shift humans by sector. I know Langley can be a dick, but I also know you can handle him. He's not stupid. He'll know this is the best option. He'll bitch, but he *will* help."

"Damn right I can deal with him, and damn straight he'll help. We're going to need tents and camping gear and tinned non-perishable goods." She was speaking more to herself now, making a mental list.

"Get the MED to source the goods. Cassie will be with you soon. Maybe she can work on the supplies?"

"Yeah, we'll fix it. You just do you."

She was referring to Bane. "I'm fine. I just want to get this sorted so I can sleep for a week."

She chuckled. "Well at least I know why I've been feeling so crappy. Fuck you, ghosts!" she said. "Hear me? Go suck on someone else's energy."

"Marika is working on summoning the Piper, so hopefully we'll have gotten rid of the ghoul problem permanently soon."

We said our goodbyes and hung up just as the mansion came into view.

Orin slid a concerned glance my way. "Are you ready for this?"

Fuck no. "Bring it."

Rivers greeted me outside Bane's chambers. It was impossible to tell what he was feeling from his expression. But his skin was paler than usual and his eyes brighter.

"Have you spoken to him?" Orin asked.

Rivers nodded then fixed his penetrating gaze on me. "He asked specifically for you."

"Me?" My pulse stalled. "Like by name?"

"Yeah. He said, *Get me Harker.*"

Bane called me Harker. He knew me? He remembered. I made to push past Rivers, but he gripped my elbow.

"He isn't Bane any longer," Rivers said. "He may remember your name, but don't get your hopes up."

He was warning me not to hope that Bane still loved me, or that he remembered us together. But how could I not? He'd asked for me by name. The flutter in my stomach wouldn't die. Not yet. Not until

I looked into his eyes and saw the absence of the neph I'd loved, for sure.

"I'll be fine." I patted Rivers's bicep. "Thank you."

"We'll be here if you need us," Orin said, his voice an empathic rumble.

But I was already inside, pushing open the door and stepping into the gloomy interior. A figure stood by the window, its back to me, bathed in the moonlight that streamed in through the glass. It was the first time I'd seen the drapes in this room open. They'd covered a set of doors leading onto a balcony. Of course, Bane would have wanted a launch pad, a mini roost of his own. Had he intended to show me it at some point? Would we have used it to go on a moonlit flight one night?

But the figure standing with his back to me wasn't Bane. His body was athletic not bulky, and his wings were ebony feathers whose tips swept the ground behind him. He turned his head to the side, highlighting his profile in silver. His nostrils flared in a Bane gesture that twisted my heart and pinched my throat. At least when confronted with Drayton, I knew there was a separate entity in the driver's seat, but what could I do about this?

"Harker."

It wasn't a question, but I answered regardless. "Yes."

"I dreamed of you."

The pinch in my throat turned into a lump. "What did you dream?" My voice was hushed, barely a whisper. But he heard me, because he turned fully to face me, silhouetted by the moon, a shadow that had once been the man I loved.

He took a step toward me, and then another, slipping out of the silver rays so the lamplight cast its glow on his heartbreakingly beautiful face. But it was his eyes that captivated me—violet and hungry and perfectly, absolutely Bane.

"I dreamed I was inside you," he said.

My breath exploded from my lips as I reached up with a trembling hand to touch his jaw. "Bane?"

He closed his eyes and a shudder ripped through him. "So many memories slipping into the vault of my mind: pain, loss, and joy, sharp and sweet." He opened his eyes. "And you. So much of you." He gripped my hand and slid it down to his chest, pressing it to his breast bone. "Here. I feel you here."

A sob expanded at the base of my throat. What was he saying?

His fingers tightened around mine. "You were important to him." His dark brows were a question mark as he scanned me with hungry curiosity. "He loved you."

He loved you. *Loved.* I pulled my hand from his grip and squeezed my eyes closed, pulling it all back, all the emotion and all the hope. Bane was no longer here. When I met Lucifer's gaze next, it was with a composed one of my own.

"Yes. We were lovers. We loved each other."

He pressed his lips together for a moment. "It must have been hard for you to let him go."

He had no idea. "Bane believed it was the right thing to do. He believed it was what Midnight needed. Midnight needed *you.*" The bitter undertone to my words would not be masked.

He picked up on it with an arched brow. "I don't blame you for resenting my presence. I'm truly sorry for your pain. But please remember that without me, there would have been no Bane."

Was he taking credit for Bane now? The simmering anger flared upwards like a stoked fire. "Bane didn't deserve to be snuffed out like that. He deserved to live."

He blinked down at me. "Serenity, I don't think you understand. Bane *isn't* dead. He will never die, because he is a part of me—his memories, his emotions." He reached up to run his fingers down my cheek. "They are now mine. He is me, just as I was him for a time."

My head reeled from his words, because the more he made sense, the more confused my emotions became.

"What are you saying?"

He blinked as if coming out of a dream. "I … I don't know." He winced and massaged his temples.

"Are you all right?"

"Harker, we need to convince Dawn to cooperate. Sunset is under attack."

It was Bane's gruff voice, his exact fucking tone. "Bane?"

Lucifer looked up at me, his expression laced with pity.

Bane … I'd heard his voice. He'd spoken directly to me. Or was I going insane? "You said something about Sunset being under attack?"

His gaze flicked to the left in recollection. "Yes. Lilith took a call from the enforcers in Sunset.

The shades have made their move into that district."

"She filled you in, then?"

He shook his head. "No. I remember."

He remembered, because he had Bane's memories. But where had the voice come from? Was hope making me hear what wasn't there? First Drayton, now Bane. Thank goodness Orin had been with me for the Drayton encounter; at least I knew that was for real.

A knock on the door interrupted us.

"Enter," Lucifer said.

The door opened and Rivers stepped in. He didn't even look at Lucifer. His attention was all for me. "Are you done?"

"If she were done, then she'd have come out," Lucifer said. His tone dropped to arctic.

Rivers shot him a flat look. "I wasn't speaking to you."

Lucifer took a menacing step toward him. "Then maybe it's time that you did."

Rivers, the man who never flinched, never showed emotion, fisted his hands at his sides. "And maybe it's time you let Serenity speak for herself."

Lucifer sighed, tucked in his chin, and exhaled, his wings drooping as he let go of his irritation. "I apologize. This must be hard for all of you. I've taken something from you, and it will take time for you to acclimatize. Harker, I believe your friend asked you a question."

"I'm fine, Rivers. I'll find you guys when I'm done."

Rivers backed out of the room and closed the door with a soft snick. I was done with this, done with being in a room with someone who'd, up until recently, made my heart sing, but now made it ache with loss. I needed to be with Ryker. I needed to crawl under the duvet with him and lose myself in his arms. I needed an epic hug from Orin and Rivers's steady, single-minded purposefulness. I needed my guys.

"You need to go to Dawn." I moved past him to the door. "You need to meet with the powers and convince them to help us. That's why you're back, that's why we let Bane go. So go do it."

He smiled thinly, a flash of anger lighting up those pretty eyes. "I'm here because this was meant to be. I'm here because this is *my* body, and yes, I plan to go to Dawn. But not alone. You will come with me."

I paused, hand on doorknob, hackles raised. "No."

He canted his head. "It's not a request."

Not a request? What the fuck? I turned slowly, deliberately, to face him. "Excuse me? You are not my boss, you are not the boss of anyone here aside from your little black-winged friends. Bane was my boss, and he left me in charge. So fuck you, *Lucifer*."

To give him credit, the dude didn't even flinch at the vitriol in my tone. Instead he smiled, calm as a midnight ocean.

"You have the only weapon that can defeat the shades," he pointed out. "You are our main advantage, and they need to know that. They need to see it in the flesh. If a neph can put her neck on the line for humanity, shame on them for hiding theirs in the sand. I've already spoken to Abigor and Malphas about this and they agree with me."

Damn. He had a valid point, but I so hated taking back my *fuck you*. But there was no denying that if Bane were here, he'd have agreed that I needed to do this.

"Next time, lead with the argument and don't issue orders. When do we leave?"

He held out his hand. "Now."

A knock at the door interrupted us.

"Come in," Lucifer called.

The door opened and Abigor stepped in, followed by Malphas. "The Black Wings are ready for your orders," Abigor said. He looked paler than usual, probably still shaken by the return of their illustrious leader.

Lucifer nodded. "Thank you for organizing that, but I need to make a short trip first."

"No." I touched his bicep without thinking, and then pulled my hand back. "Go speak to the Black Wings first. They've waited long enough to have you back. They deserve to see you, to hear words of encouragement. I need to freshen up anyway and check up on a few things."

Lucifer studied me for a long beat. "Very well."

Very well? Urgh. Bane would have said, *Fucking do it*, or, *Are you questioning me, Harker?* This guy was so … proper. Every moment with him took a chunk out of my memories of Bane. I needed to get away from him.

Malphas followed me out into the corridor. "Serenity. We didn't know. None of us knew."

"Yeah, I figured."

"But we're grateful for what you did to bring him back. He's determined to get Abbadon back. Oath be damned." He smiled. "Once the White Wings join us, we will outnumber the shade army, and with your help, we'll be able to bring them to heel. They can't infect us, and if your plan is a success, they will lose potential hosts. The odds will be evened out."

For the first time since I'd ripped open the veil and released Asher and his army, I felt a delicious spark of optimism, that, yes, we could get the upper hand in this battle.

"Well, let's hope freeing Lucifer and losing Bane was worth it then. He better have the silver tongue you guys say he does."

I left him hovering outside the room and headed off toward mine. I needed to wash away this last half hour and get my head straight.

"Langley has taken on transport responsibility and speaking to the families of the affected," Ava said. "Cassie is picking up supplies. We should have the first lot of humans settled at Respite in the next couple of hours."

"Good. That's really good. Once that's done, we can start working on sector three. It's closest to Respite. We'll also have an idea of how much space we have to play with by then."

We wouldn't be able to save all the humans, but

we'd cut the shade host options in half, and once we had the Piper and the ghosts were gone, maybe the humans left outside of Respite would be able to fight infection more effectively.

"Okay, I'll check in with you soon." Ava hung up.

I shrugged on a clean long-sleeved top and gathered my hair up into a low ponytail. My body ached and throbbed with power. It had only been a day since I'd expelled a shitload at the hospital, but it was back again, thrumming under my skin, eager to get out.

"Serenity?"

Ambrosius? I switched to aether-sight to find him standing by the bed. "Hey. How are things going with the summoning spell search?"

"We're working on it." He studied me intently. "What about you?"

"Me?"

He walked toward me, that intense look still on his face. "How are you feeling?"

"I'm fine. Just about to head off to Dawn with Ba—Lucifer." Shit, now he was looking at me with sympathy, and it was the last thing I needed. "Don't. I'm fine, okay. I'm going to be fine. And once we have the White Wings on board, it will all be worth it."

He nodded. "Oleander is about to leave for the clifftop house, and I will go with him. The library there is vast, and two heads are better than one."

"Good. Getting rid of the ghosts is essential to the overall plan."

"I know and we will. The Piper is real. I know

this, I just do not recall the summoning ritual, but it is out there, and we will find it."

"I know you'll do your best. Also, while you're there, look for anything we can find on these shades. Any titbit of information that might be lying around."

"I doubt there will be anything. I believe they may predate the written word, that they predate even the winged."

"Then anything on how we might be able to remove an entity from a host without forcible expulsion or extermination."

His brow crinkled. "What is this about, Serenity?"

I massaged my temple; my headache had returned. "Drayton. I know he's still alive, trapped inside Xavier, and today, Orin and I saw Xavier and we heard Drayton. He spoke to us."

"Xavier spoke to you …" Ambrosius looked confused.

"No. I mean, yes. He spoke to us but with Drayton's voice, the exact inflection, and he warned us not to kill Xavier." The skeptical look on his face made my head hurt more. "Look, just do it, okay. Please. I can't explain it, but Orin was there, he heard it too, and we … we just need to find a way to help him, okay?"

Ambrosius shrugged. "I will keep that in mind when going through the texts, but Serenity, our priority is the Piper."

"I know."

He nodded and then stepped through the wall. Gone. I slipped out of aether-sight and reached for my boots. A knock on the door was followed by Ryker's scent as he entered the room.

"I don't like this. We don't know him," Ryker said as I pulled on my kicks.

"Hello to you too." Ignoring the itch and bite in my limbs, I straightened to face him. "I assume the *him* you're referring to is Lucifer?"

"You assume correctly."

"Bane would have wanted me to do this. It's why he left in the first place."

Ryker pinched the bridge of his nose. "It's not Lucifer I have a problem with. It's the White Wings I don't trust. He shouldn't ask you to go with him."

"We don't have a choice."

"I'm coming with you."

"No. That's not a good idea."

He cupped my shoulders and looked down into my face with his crystal-blue eyes before pulling me into his arms. "Dammit, Harker. How can I keep you safe if I'm here and you're there?"

I relaxed in his embrace and reveled in his hands running up and down my back. His fingers threaded through my hair, and he cradled the back of my head with his huge, axe-wielding hand. I leaned back into his palm and gazed up at him, my big, blond, blue-eyed, crazy axe guy. He'd taken me under his wing from day one. Shielding me, keeping my secret, and then slipping effortlessly into role of best friend and snuggle buddy, and somewhere along the way, he'd taken residence in my heart. Somewhere along the way I'd fallen for him. It wasn't a passionate, I-need-to-tear-off-your-clothes kind of love like it had been with Bane. This was a steady thrum in my veins. It was a promise to have and to hold.

"Everything will be all right," he said with confidence.

His lips were tantalizingly close, and the urge to kiss him was sudden and fierce. I inhaled sharply, and his attention fell to my mouth. I reached up to touch his chin and trace his bottom lip with my fingertips. His eyelids fluttered closed for a brief moment, and the muscles in his arms jumped. I was tired, so tired of fighting my wants, and every day I kept my mouth shut was another missed opportunity.

"I need to tell you something." My voice was hoarse. "I don't know what's going to happen over the next few hours, or days, but I need you to know."

"Serenity …" He searched my face, trying to gauge what I was about to say.

Bane had said they loved me, Ryker included, but if it wasn't the kind of love I had for him then I didn't want to see the pity on his face. I closed my eyes. "I know you care about me and that we're friends, but it's more than that for me, has been for a long while. It just took losing Bane to accept it." I opened my eyes and stared into his dilating pupils. "I love you, Ryker … more than a friend should."

His breath hitched and he dipped his head.

A loud knock on the door had us springing apart. My face burned and twin spots of color highlighted his cheekbones. He felt the same. In that unguarded moment it was written all over his face. My heart soared.

Orin popped his head around the door. "Lucifer's ready to leave."

I nodded. "Okay."

"We'll finish this conversation later," Ryker said, back in control.

I nodded and followed Orin out of the room, butterflies fluttering in my chest with the knowledge of what had almost happened.

In the corridor outside, I took a left toward the roost, but Orin took my hand and tugged me right. Oh, yeah. Of course. It wasn't Bane we were going to meet.

"Where is he?"

"Outside. Flexing his wings. They're pretty impressive. The other Black Wings are psyched to have him back. I have no idea what they talked about in their meeting but they seem pumped. Funny, considering they aren't actually allowed to interfere in human affairs."

"But they *can* protect themselves if the shades attack them."

"Yeah."

We took the stairs to the foyer, and a blast of cold air swept to meet us. The double doors were open and voices could be heard outside.

It sounded like a crowd, as if … "Don't tell me he has an audience."

"Okay, I won't."

"Can you tell the others about Drayton. Just tell them what we heard and saw?"

"No problem."

We stepped outside and into a throng of Black Wings. Feathers brushed my face and my arms, and boots crunched on gravel as bodies parted to let me through. They were big and menacing and powerful, and yet they were useless to the humans. An army that could only go up against the shades in the name of protecting themselves, and this was why Lucifer was here, to get us an army to take the focus off the humans. Yeah, it helped to remind myself why we'd set him free. It helped to give it all purpose.

And there was the man himself, dressed in black ... Bane's black shirt. It fit perfectly and didn't look as if he was about to burst out of it. His dark hair had been swept off his face and into a low ponytail accentuating the perfect-cut features that combined to make up his visage. The only part of him recognizable as Bane were his eyes, and they were fixed on me now, drinking me in as I strode toward him.

"Are you ready to leave now?" he asked. His voice was still deep like Bane's had been, but the gruff edge was gone, smoothed away by the transformation.

"Yeah, let's get this over with." I stepped up to him, expecting him to open his arms, so used to Bane simply scooping me up. He blinked, taken aback, and anger rose up in my chest, sudden and fiery. "What? You got a problem with touching me? You're gonna need to carry me, genius."

It was uncalled for and harsh, but it felt good ... for about a second. I pinched the bridge of my nose, ignoring the shocked chatter behind me. "I didn't mean to snap."

He took a step closer to me and then tucked a loose strand of my hair behind my ear. "I understand."

My eyes burned. "Yeah, well, it would help if you were more of a dick."

His laughter was a gruff, gravelly sound that was so Bane it made me ache to hold him, even if it was just pretend.

"I'll try my best to work on that," Lucifer said. He gently tugged me into his arms, and I glanced over my shoulder to see Orin incline his head. *It'll be all right*, that gesture said.

"It will be all right," Lucifer echoed. "Now, hold on."

"Wait, you were gone before Arcadia was born, how will you even know where to go?"

He smiled sadly. "I just do."

Bane ... He knew because of Bane's memories. I swallowed the lump in my throat, wrapped my arms around him, pressed my face into his neck, and closed my eyes. The air shifted, his wings stroked the air, and then we were flying.

The world beyond my eyelids turned red and then orange.

"We're approaching Dawn," Lucifer said.

"They have wards. We need to be careful."

"I see them." He swerved and dipped. I opened my eyes and looked over my shoulder. The world was a haze of pink, yellow, and green—a rainbow dome covering the pearly gates. How much power had it taken to build this ward?

"Combined divine power," Lucifer said. "It's solid. There won't be any getting in without them allowing it."

We were getting close now and dropping

altitude. Something glinted at us from beyond the ward and then a *whooshing* sound filled the air. A bolt of metal sliced past my ear, stopping my breath and tightening my muscles. Lucifer banked left.

"What the heck was that?"

"I don't—"

The air was filled with the *whoosh* and slice of bolts cutting through the sky toward us. Lucifer went into auto-flight, dipping, diving, banking, and rising to avoid the shots. But he was carrying me, and it must have been throwing off his balance, because there was a definite wobble to every move he made no matter how expertly done.

Shit.

I pressed my lips to his ear. "We need to get onto the ground."

He nodded curtly. "Hold on!"

And then we were diving like a fucking bullet headed for the tarmac. There was no way he'd be able to stop. No way could he pull up in time. We were going to go straight through the earth and out the other side. A scream locked in my throat. I held on for dear life while the air roaring in my ears joined the rush of blood in my head. And then my whole body jerked in his arms as we came to an abrupt halt.

My feet kissed the ground, but Lucifer didn't release me. Good, because my knees felt like jelly. He cradled me, whispering in a language I didn't understand. His hands smoothed down my hair and slowly my pulse stopped trying to claw its way out of my veins.

Boots slapped the ground and Lucifer's grip on me tightened. I pushed at his chest, wanting to see who was approaching, and reluctantly he released me.

The gates were open and a large White Wing stood there with several other White Wings flanking him. His golden beard winked in the sunlight.

Michael shook his head in wonder. "Lucifer? Is that really you?"

"In the flesh," Lucifer said.

"This can't be true. You can't be here."

"And yet I am," Lucifer said. "Now, don't you want to know why and how?"

Michael's chest rose and fell erratically, and then he stepped through the wards and walked toward us. "I'm listening."

Lucifer paced the tarmac, hands on hips, chin tucked in. His wings trailed behind him, formidable and gleaming obsidian in the butter-yellow rays of the sun. The wards glowed in front of us, shielding waiting guards toting bolt guns aimed at the ground. Michael had retreated to the hub of Dawn to speak to the Powers and fill them in on Lucifer's return. He'd been gone a while.

"What is taking so long?" Lucifer asked. His boots made fresh tracks on the dusty tarmac as he shifted trajectory.

It was a rhetorical question but what the heck. "I don't know."

He glared at me, the first real flash of temper I'd seen from the calm and collected Black Wing. It was kinda comforting and a grin tugged at my lips.

He exhaled through his nose. "They should be dragging us through the wards, begging me to tell the story of how I tricked them."

Arrogant much? "Or maybe they just don't care anymore." The words just popped out, but they made sense.

It *had* been over a century, and while at first the White Wings may have been bothered by Lucifer's disappearance, they'd moved on, come to an agreement with the Black Wings, and created Arcadia. So much had changed. Maybe Lucifer just didn't hold as much value to them anymore. Ice trickled through my veins. Had we made a mistake in choosing him over Bane?

I looked up to find him watching me. He'd stopped pacing now, and was just … staring at me. "You wish I were gone."

I rolled my eyes. "Hardly a revelation."

He sighed. "I will not continue to apologize for my existence, Harker."

My temper flared. "Don't. Don't call me that, and don't say it … like that."

He made a sound of exasperation and turned away. His shoulders were obscured by the rise of his wings. Why hadn't he put them away? Bane always tucked his away when not in flight. And what did I care anyway?

Movement at the gate was followed by Michael's return. He passed through the shimmering wards and walked toward us, shaking his head solemnly.

Lucifer looked incredulous. "They won't see me?"

"You fake your disappearance and then you turn up here demanding an audience with the Powers. What did you expect?" Michael said.

"I would have thought their curiosity would have been enough to grant me an audience."

"You're lucky you haven't been shot through with a bolt where you stand," Michael said. "I can't believe it. All this time you were here, right under our noses. You were here in Dawn, working for us as Bane, and we never knew."

"To be fair, neither did I."

"What was it like?" Michael asked. "What was it like being … gone?"

His gaze grew distant. "Like a dream. Like a long sleep. It feels like only yesterday that I closed my eyes, and yet so much has changed."

"And now you're back and you want our help."

"No. I just want you to do what you pledged to do—protect humanity. We all want the same thing, although our methods may be at odds. You want to protect humanity physically by taking their free will and turning them into puppets. We want to allow them to flourish and evolve and protect the precious gift of free will gifted to them by our creator."

A dark shadow passed across Michael's face. "Humans are their own worst enemies, and left to their own devices they will ultimately destroy each other."

"And that would be their journey. One they should be permitted to take. It is what God would have wanted."

"And yet he isn't here, is he? He left us to watch over them, and he retreated to goodness knows where. He left his favored creation in our hands and we watched while they abused the free will he had gifted them. They do not deserve it, and deep down you know it."

"So instead you make them your slaves? How

does getting them to serve you count as protecting them? It seems perfectly selfish to me."

"We give them a safe home. We provide peace and harmony, and if they pay for this with servitude, then what is the harm in that? We are White Wings, we are God's first creation."

Well, that just wasn't accurate. "Not if the shades are to be believed."

He glared at me. "What do you mean?"

I shrugged. "The shades predate you. And I'm pretty sure the humans are just a means to an end for them. They need the hosts to get to *you*. It's the winged they have a grudge against. It's you they want to end. They'll be coming for you once they have the manpower, which, if you don't help us, they will have sooner rather than later. So, how about you stop hiding and get out there and fucking help us to stop them."

Michael averted his gaze, and I saw the first shadow of doubt on his face.

"The shades were always going to spill into our world," Lucifer said. "And Merlin and I did what we could to prepare ourselves for it. The weapon is here now, at the perfect time when needed." He swept an arm toward me. "The Powers need to see her. They need to know what she can do."

Michael looked shifty and Lucifer tensed.

"You did tell them about her, didn't you? You told them about the weapon inside her?"

Michael's gaze swept over me, and his eyes softened. "No. I didn't, and if you're wise you'll keep that under wraps for as long as possible."

Lucifer balked. "Hide our main advantage?

Why would we do that?"

My mind was whirring, making connections, and when the pieces fell into place, Michael's reluctance made sense. How had Lucifer and I not come to the same conclusion? "The weapon was made of God's grace—the only thing that could kill a Black Wing ... that could kill a winged. If I'm the weapon, then it means that I can kill the White Wings too."

Michael's smile was close-lipped. "If they find out. If you set foot in Dawn, then you won't be permitted to leave. They won't allow such a powerful weapon to remain in the Black Wings' hands."

Lucifer turned away in exasperation. "Fine. But even without the weapon it doesn't change the fact that we need to join forces to band against a common threat. A threat that is using the humans as cannon fodder to get to us."

"The shades are not a threat to us," Michael said softly, although he didn't sound too convinced. "They cannot infect us, and Dawn is warded against them with our divine power. It seems the threat is entirely to you." He locked gazes with Lucifer. "And you have a weapon to fight it with."

"And what about the humans out there in Midnight and Sunset? Do you not have a duty to protect them?" Lucifer asked.

"We have a duty to the humans who joined us, who gave us their will and became silvered, and we will not risk their lives to save the resistors. The tally of humans outside of Dawn has dropped dramatically, and we have the numbers we need to win our wager."

So that was their ploy? Sit things out and wait

for the century to be over, and when Arcadia rejoined the rest of the world, they could stake claim to all of humanity. But there was something they hadn't thought about.

"While you hide, the rest of Arcadia could fall, and then when the magic around Arcadia fails, when you are finally reunited with the rest of the world, what then? The shades will still be here, and they will have a billion fresh humans to choose from, to build their army, to procreate, and to take you down." I had no idea about the procreation bit, but it seemed to have an effect on him because his eyes widened in horror at the thought. "So you see, sitting back and doing nothing isn't going to give you the advantage. All you're doing is delaying the inevitable, but if you join us now, we can cut the head off the serpent before he grows any more. The White Wings don't need to know about my abilities, not yet. Not until it's time for me to burn the shades into oblivion. And trust me, once they see that, they won't try putting their hands on me."

"You know she's right, Michael," Lucifer said. "We need to work together or this world that God created will be taken from us completely."

From the look on Michael's face, if it had been up to him, we'd be getting that audience about now. But it wasn't, and he quickly shuttered his emotions. "I'm sorry, there's nothing I can do. The Powers have made their decision. They have forsaken the humans outside of Dawn. The humans who turned their back on the White Wings are no longer our concern. We must protect the silvered at all costs."

We weren't going to get anywhere here. I had

neph shadows to slice off and a Piper to summon. I turned to Lucifer. "Let's go. We're wasting our time. We're on our own."

Lucifer's jaw ticked, but he nodded and held out his arms to me.

I stepped into his embrace, closing my eyes and imagining, for a brief moment, that it was Bane holding me. Lucifer's arms tightened around me.

"One more thing," Michael said. "As a Black Wing, you aren't permitted to aid the humans. No interference, remember?" He winced at the words. Words probably passed to him by the Powers. "As Bane you were not yourself, and so the Powers have magnanimously agreed to excuse you, but you are Lucifer once more, and therefore, you must abide by the rules of our wager."

Lucifer's biceps flexed. I glanced up at his face, sharp features cut in stone.

"Fuck you, Michael. Fuck all of you."

My pulse skipped in shock, and a chuckle spilled from my lips. His wings flapped, and we were airborne.

"You thought that was funny?" he asked, his lips close to my ear.

My mirth evaporated. "No, it's just … that was so …"

"Bane?" he asked, his voice low.

Pain lanced through my heart. "Yeah."

"I know."

"Stand still." I placed a hand on Rivers's shoulder to

turn him slightly, putting him directly in the path of the spotlight. His shadow stretched out behind him on the lounge floor. Orin, Ryker, and Rivers stood by the window. We'd moved the sofas back and locked the door to the lounge. If this shadow slicing worked, then we could start on the rest of the nephs in the building. And once they were done, then it would be time to call in the Lupin and get them sliced too. Right now, the beast men were out in the district, helping us to keep the humans safe. It would be a challenge to liberate every neph of his or her shadow, but it was one I was up for if it meant keeping them out of shade clutches.

"Just get it over with," Rivers said.

"Nervous?" I teased.

"Do I look nervous?"

I glanced up at his deadpan face. "Okay, ice dude." I released him and stepped back. My daggers appeared in my hands. "What about now?"

He shook his head and looked away. Yeah, there was no shaking Rivers. As soon as I'd asked for a volunteer, he'd stepped up. But despite my bravado, my palms were sweating. If I could have tried this on myself first then I would have, but that idea had been vetoed by the guys. My abilities were too important to risk losing, and if something did go wrong, if Ambrosius had got his facts wrong, then they couldn't take the risk of messing with my power.

"And how do you do this?" Cassie asked. There was a definite mocking edge to her voice.

Wiping my clammy palms on my jeans, I fixed a confident smile on my face. "Ambrosius said I could just slice."

"So do it," Rivers said. "Slice."

I crouched on the ground, checked the tremble in my hands, and made the cut, keeping close to Rivers's heels, and fuck me sideways, the inky black shadow began to contract and then winked out completely.

"Well that was weird," Cassie said.

"You okay, Rivers?" Ryker asked.

"Fine. Cassie can go next." He stepped away from me.

"No way," Cassie said. "Ryker can go next."

"I trust you, Serenity." Ryker took Rivers's spot and Orin adjusted the light. "Do it."

Taking a deep breath, I set to liberation.

Five minutes later they were all shadow free, which meant the damn shades couldn't infect them. It was as if someone had removed a boulder off my chest. Ryker was already on the phone to Gregory, the Lupin leader, and Orin was dialing Adam, the Sanguinata liaison.

Cassie pressed a drink into my hand. "You did good."

I'd just finished slicing off my own shadow, and it felt weird. *I* felt weird. "Do you feel lighter? Like you've lost weight?"

"Yeah, I thought I was imagining it."

"Weird."

She licked her lips. "So have you spoken to Orin since our chat?"

Heat climbed up my chest as the memory of the kiss in the van bloomed in my mind's eye. "Um, yeah. He drove me to the cemetery."

She ducked her head. "Are you going to … Are

you going to get together?"

Guilt mingled with empathy. Yeah, she'd fucked up with Orin, but she still cared about him. But the things she'd said, the way she'd put him down. I couldn't forgive that. Or maybe I was just making excuses to be with him, to clear my conscience. Thank God Cassie and I had never been close, because that would be awkward—friend code and all that.

"Yes."

She blew out a breath. "Thanks for being honest."

"Always."

"Adam said he'd swing by in an hour." Orin tucked his phone back into his jeans pocket.

"Gregory is on his way now," Ryker added.

We may have failed in convincing the White Wings to join us, but a bunch of humans were safe in Respite, and I'd just effectively sliced the shadows off four nephs. Despite the White Wings turning their back on us, we were succeeding in gaining an advantage over the shades.

I slugged back the amber liquid in my glass. "Let's get this done."

The next two days passed in a haze of patrols and reading. The Latin books were passed to me. It seemed like my little language skill may have come from the power inside me and it was good to be of more use than blasting shades, but the lack of shade action meant the power inside me was building.

When I wasn't reading, I was over the border in Sunset expelling shades from their human hosts. Since finding out the shades had moved into Sunset, we'd scheduled patrols to cover the district, providing one MPD officer per SPD unit. The Lupin had picked up the slack in Midnight, filling in where we were lacking. The scourge were back, attacking wherever they could and stretching our resources, which I guess was the shades' plan. Overwhelm and distract. Dorian had done the minimum. He'd provided a small team headed up by Adam, the Sanguinata who we'd met when we'd entered the House Games a few weeks ago. Then he'd cloistered himself in his moat-surrounded castle, and we hadn't heard from him since, the bastard.

So far, there'd been only a handful of infections reported in Sunset. The citizens there seemed more aware of changes in their mental state and willingly brought themselves to the drop-in center that had been set up. The SPD had been quick to inform district citizens about the threat. Pamphlets providing information on signs and symptoms to watch for were circulated, and it was working. The shades were failing to get their hooks into their hosts. I'd made three trips to carry out expulsions, but expulsions weren't the same as incinerating the fuckers, and I desperately needed the release of a few kills.

My temper was shorter, and both Orin and Ryker had been on the end of the sharp side of my tongue. This wasn't me. Something had to be done about it. Ambrosius was at the clifftop house with Oleander, but as soon as he got back, I'd get his advice on what was happening. My daimon was ominously silent, and aside from everything else, this one fact was worrying.

Meanwhile, Lucifer may not have been able to convince the Powers, but he'd been a wizard at rousing the Black Wings. They couldn't interfere directly, but he'd suggested that they place themselves in positions where they may be attacked. If they were attacked, they could retaliate, right?

For the first time since I'd met Abigor and Malphas, I'd seen a new fire in their eyes and caught a glimpse of the warriors beneath the impotence.

The Black Wings were out there now, broken into units and patrolling sectors one and two in the hope that shades would attack them. Sector three had been partially evacuated and Respite was full. It was all we could do until we found the summoning spell for the Piper.

"Are you going to finish that or not?" Orin asked.

I blinked out of my thoughts and stared at the cinnamon roll in my hand. It was still warm from the oven, and I didn't even care about the crumbs on my duvet. Stuffing my face with baked goods in bed, courtesy of Orin, was just the ticket right now. He'd made me breakfast—rolls and freshly brewed coffee. I was rumpled from sleep, and probably looked like I'd been dragged backward through a hedge, but the way he was looking at me you'd think I'd just stepped onto the catwalk. I wrinkled my nose in an effort to defuse the sudden anticipatory tension.

He chuckled and reached across the bed to wipe crumbs from my face, his fingers lingering at the corner of my mouth. "Piglet," he said fondly.

"Enabler." I grinned.

His eyes darkened, and he swept a thumb across my lips. "I love cooking for you."

Warmth flooded me. "I love it when you do."

"I love watching you eat."

"I love it when you feed me."

He broke off a piece of cinnamon roll and held it to my lips. I took it in my mouth and kept my gaze trained on his while I did it. I licked the tips of his fingers before he could withdraw, and his breathing quickened.

"Finish what's in your mouth," he said hoarsely.

The tension was back and my body went into high alert. Yes. This was it. This was our breaking point, the tipping point. Pull away or submit? But he made the decision for me by grasping the back of my neck, leaning in, and devouring my mouth with his butterscotch lips. I kicked off the covers and pulled him on top of me, the whole of him—huge, hard, and fucking mine. Skin, I needed to feel skin. The T-shirt had to go.

"Wait." He reared up, staring down at me through unfathomable eyes. "I want to savor this."

He ran his hands down my torso, over my breasts, his palms teasing my nipples and skimming my stomach. My back arched almost involuntarily into his caress, and his breath hissed through his clenched teeth.

"Fucking hell, Serenity." He slipped his hands under my bed-T and slid it up, caressing the sides of my breasts.

Was that my moan, eager and desperate? "Orin … Please …" This was painful. Slow and painful and evil. "Please."

He smiled, and a wicked gleam lit up his stormy eyes. "I need to feel you. Taste you."

My stomach flipped hard, and a throb started low and wanton between my thighs. Air kissed my skin as he peeled off my shirt, and then his mouth descended on my neck. His tongue flicked out to lick and his lips brushed my skin in feather-light kisses, trailing down to my breasts, but skirting the peak, tongue making lazy circles, forcing my body to tighten and beg and moan before he finally closed his warm, wet mouth over my nipple and began to draw. My hips bucked, and my legs opened to make room for him. The world spun as he explored me with delicate intensity. My lungs were too tight, my body a knot of need. Silk between my fingers, velvet against my thighs. He was naked, his body sliding against mine, taut muscle beneath my fingertips as he found my wet core and pushed me to the edge.

"Please, Orin. Please."

"Yes." Hand on my forehead to hold me still, he locked gazes with me. "Look at me, Serenity. I need to see you." And then he entered me. Inch by delicious inch, he stretched me. Big … He was big, thick, and there was no more thought, only the sensations wrung free from my sensitized flesh as we claimed each other.

"That was …" My legs were still quivering and every

part of my body was singing. He'd given each part of me attention. Who knew that the insides of my wrists could be an erogenous zone? He stroked my arm, his gaze trailing across my face.

"I've been wanting to do that for … a long time," he said.

I smiled. "Yeah? Well, you had me fooled."

He propped himself up on his elbow. "Look. I know how things are. I know how you feel about the others, and that's okay."

I ran a hand over his smoothly shaven jaw. "I'm glad. I'd never want to hurt you. And I want you to know that the way I feel about you is unique to us." I leaned up to kiss his lips. "No one can replicate that."

Orin closed his eyes and touched my forehead with his. "Good to know."

Cassie's warning circulated in my mind. "I promise I'll never push you away, or make you feel unwanted. I know with Cassie and Killion … You weren't happy and—"

He tensed. "You're not Cassie, and Ryker and Rivers are my friends. Killion was an abusive arsehole, and Cassie choosing to be with him was insulting."

I sat up. "So, you wouldn't have minded if she'd been with someone else other than Killion?"

He shrugged. "I'm not sure. She wanted an open relationship, and I wanted her, so I agreed. Then Killion came back onto the scene, and it hurt to see her with him."

"Does it hurt you to think about me with Bane?"

He blinked down at me. "No, I just … I was

jealous of him. I wanted you too." He smoothed my hair back. "There's something about you, Serenity. Not just your cambion nature, but you. You have the biggest heart, and empathy … You have so much empathy, and I know that my heart will be safe in your hands. I know you would never intentionally hurt me. And if it means being with you, then I don't mind having to share."

His hand slipped down my side and over the curve of my hip to settle between my thighs. He stroked me, sending shivers up my spine.

"I'm not on patrol for another hour." His tone was gravelly with need.

"A-huh." I shifted my hips, eager for him to take the next step.

"So …"

I licked my lips. "Yes, please."

He smiled, flashing his even, white teeth, and then he slid his finger into my heat.

Showered and dressed, I headed for the door. I was on Sunset patrol tonight with the SPD. It was gonna be weird working with the guys again, especially since I was going to be in charge, but there was no denying that I was looking forward to seeing the old gang again. Shame about the circumstances.

"Serenity?" Ambrosius's voice came from in front of me.

I slipped into aether-sight to find him disheveled and bright-eyed, right in my face.

"Whoa, personal space check, Ambrosius."

"We found it," he said. "We found the summoning spell."

My pulse tripped. "You did? You're sure?"

He nodded. "Oleander found it at the cliff house. He's on his way back now with Abigor. I wanted to tell you first. I need to tell Marika now, so we can get set up."

It was happening so fast. "Set up?"

"The summoning requires some prep—an arcane circle using the correct symbols. We'll need a large space, but we should be good to go in about an hour."

"An hour?" Okay, now I was sounding like an echo. Pull it together. This is what we'd been hoping for, the final nudge we needed in our advantage over the shades. I'd have to get a couple of Protectorate to fill in for me with the SPD, because this took precedence. This could turn the tide in our favor. "Okay, let me grab the guys and I'll meet you in the training room. It's spacious, so we should set up there."

He slipped through the wall and was gone.

Orin was still on patrol, but Ryker and Rivers should be about somewhere. The training room would need to be my first port of call; Cassie was giving the human unit a workout, and maybe one of the guys was with her. We needed to clear out the room anyway.

I rounded the corridor and ran smack bang into a solid wall of muscle. Hands grabbed my arms to stall my backward stumble.

"You're in a hurry?" Lucifer's honeyed voice trickled over my senses.

I stepped away from him, away from the undertone of familiar scent. "Oleander found the summoning spell. I need to find the others."

"The spell to summon the Piper?"

"Yeah."

He pressed his lips together. "Make sure he also has the counter spell, the one to send him back."

Abbadon had known who the Piper was, but hadn't gone into detail, and it was obvious from the shadow that had fallen over Lucifer's face that he knew what we would be dealing with too.

The urge to understand swelled within me. "What is he? What is Death really?"

Lucifer blew out a breath and shrugged. "A rumor. Nothing more. Never anything concrete. A few of us caught wind of his existence not long after the dawn of man. We went to the creator to ask who this entity was that plagued mankind, but we were ordered to leave him be. To never go where he walked."

"Why? Why would God warn you away?"

Lucifer shrugged. "I have no idea. None of us do. But we heard tales of his reaping. He walked the battlefields, and wound his way through the towns riddled with disease. He came when summoned, but lingered until expelled by the arcane. But as time passed and magic was weakened by technology, he was forgotten."

"Magic is weak outside of Arcadia?"

He sighed. "I do not know. It has been over a century since I walked the earth. But when I left, yes, magic had been weakened. Humanity had begun to lose faith, almost as if the creator's withdrawal had somehow communicated itself to his children via the aether that touches us all."

"So, we need to have a counter spell, and we need to keep an eye on Death."

"Yes."

"Are you going to be okay being in the room when we summon him? I mean, you promised God that you wouldn't cross his path …"

"And *He* promised to watch over us. I think the shelf life on those promises has expired."

I nodded. "Okay. I'm going to go find the guys."

"You mean Ryker, Rivers, and Orin?"

Those were my guys. "Yeah."

He looked at me strangely, and my scalp prickled under the scrutiny. What was he doing in this part of the mansion, anyway? "Were you looking for someone?"

He blinked down at me. "I guess I was."

"What's that supposed to mean?"

"Your room is on this floor?"

"Yeah."

"I suppose in that case I was looking for you."

He was freaking me out. "You *suppose*?"

He smiled wryly. "I decided to take a walk, get the lay of the land, and my feet led me here."

Not his feet, Bane's feet. Bane's memories. I couldn't do this right now. I couldn't remember him. "Well you found me, but we have work to do, so how about you find Malphas instead? Make sure the other Black Wings stay out of the training room for the rest of the afternoon. We need to keep this small—just the Order, the primary nephs, Ava, you, Malphas, and

Abigor. Oh, and Oleander—he did find the summoning spell, after all."

He nodded curtly. "You're a natural at this."

I arched a brow.

He grinned, and the absence of fangs made my heart hurt. "Leading, Harker. You're a natural at leading."

"Yeah? Then why are you still standing here?"

He backed up a step and then turned on his heel and headed back the way he'd come. A minute. I needed just one minute for him to be gone and take his scent with him. Being around him was disconcerting—a constant reminder of what I'd lost. Best to avoid him whenever possible, at least until the loss wasn't so raw. And when would that be? Drayton had been gone months, but it still hurt to think about him, and now, knowing he was trapped inside his own body, the agitation was ten times worse. Thank goodness things were moving forward with the shade predicament. Action was the only cure for a bruised heart.

It was time to summon the Piper.

The room was brightly lit and the arcane symbol had been painted onto the ground. Rivers had assisted with the runes, ones that the Order hadn't seen before, but Rivers seemed to instinctively understand. They'd glowed briefly as he'd drawn them onto the ground. The Order stood around the circle, eyes closed, holding hands. At a glance they looked calm and composed, but a closer inspection revealed the cracks.

Perspiration glistened on Marika's forehead, and her companions were showing the strain as well—mouths were twisted, brows furrowed, and knees trembled. This was no easy feat, whatever they were doing. However, they were drawing arcane power to channel into the circle and it was having a negative effect on them.

Long minutes ticked by, and then one of the Order members fell to her knees, bringing her comrades down with her, but they didn't break contact, and none of them opened their eyes. Oleander shifted from foot to foot, the book that contained the summoning ritual clutched to his chest like a shield.

I looked to Rivers. "This isn't working. It's hurting them."

"The runes are powerful," he said. "Give them a moment to draw what they need."

To my left, Lucifer stared at the circle intently as if he could force it to life through will alone. And then a collective sigh went up, and the Order tucked in their chins, shoulders sagging. The symbols lit up one by one, as if in some secret arcane order, like a code that only the Order could tap into.

"Here we go," Rivers whispered.

It was happening, the damn thing was charging. The Order pulled each other to their feet and began to hum, a low-level sound that had the hairs on the back of my neck shifting with unease. The air was suddenly electric, crackling with power, and then lightning lanced down from the ceiling and smashed into the center of the circle. A shockwave flared outward, smacking me in the chest and propelling me backward into the body behind me.

We hit the ground, the body breaking my fall. We hadn't been the only ones hit; everyone within range was down.

"Shit." I glanced over my shoulder at Ryker, who had his arms around me. "You okay?"

"Yeah. I got you." His gaze slid from my face to the center of the room. "Motherfucker."

A figure stood in the circle, head bowed, naked except for a pair of loose black pants. His hair was long, no short. Dark, no it was blond. I blinked and rubbed my eyes. A woman? No, it was definitely a guy—a tan-skinned, dark-haired guy. He raised his head and looked straight at me with his almond eyes.

"Death's a woman?" Ryker whispered.

But I was trapped in Death's obsidian gaze. He cocked his head and crooked his finger, and, by God, I was on my feet and taking the first steps toward that blazing circle. Someone hooked me around the waist and pulled me back.

"Snap out of it, Serenity." Rivers's voice was an icy slap.

Shit, what the heck? I shook my head. I'd been about to breach the circle.

"He's smaller than I expected," Rivers said.

The guy was huge. What was he talking about? Wait. "Ryker, what do you see?"

Ryker tore his attention from Death and focused on me. "What?"

"What is in the circle?"

"A woman." His cheeks grew pink. "A naked woman."

Rivers's arm flexed around me. "I see a guy, small, thin, unshaven."

Lucifer joined us. "I do believe Death is mutable."

"What do *you* see?"

He blinked several times and then looked away. "It doesn't matter. What matters is how we'll keep track of an entity that appears different to us all."

I glanced at Malphas and Abigor, who had also averted their gazes. There was something going on here that the Black Wings weren't sharing with us.

"We tether him," Marika said.

Death arched a brow and crossed his arms.

"Why isn't he saying anything?" Orin asked.

Death smirked.

Marika caught her bottom lip between her teeth. "I don't know. I think the circle is simply a doorway, a peek into his world. Right now he's standing in that doorway, but to allow him to interact with our world, we'd need to pull him through and tether him."

"And we do that how?" Lucifer asked.

It was Oleander who answered. He was poring over the pages in the book that had revealed the summoning ritual. "One of us has to volunteer to anchor him—no, wait, not volunteer, be chosen." He looked up, his face pale. "We have to let him choose his anchor."

Death's gaze was on me again. He looked … hungry. My throat was suddenly dry. "And what does this anchoring involve?"

"This symbol." Oleander held up the book. "We have to cut it into the person Death chooses, and it will allow us to pull him through."

"It's a binding rune," Rivers said. "A pretty powerful one."

Oleander blinked up at him. "You know a lot about runes."

"It's a gift," Rivers said, deadpan.

"I don't like this," Orin interrupted. "Why is he staring at Serenity?"

"Maybe he wants to fuck her too," Cassie muttered.

Rivers shot her a lethal look. But my stomach turned because he *was* staring at me intently, with purpose. Please do not pick me, pick someone else, anyone else. It was a horrible thing to think but it was a reflex thought, and once it was scrolling through my mind, it wouldn't dissipate.

Oleander walked up to the boundary and held the book up so Death could see the symbol, which took up a whole page. Death stared at it and nodded, his expression suddenly all business.

Oleander stepped back to allow Death a view of the room. Death's focus shifted to me once more, but then he smiled, raised a hand, and pointed straight at Marika. Her gasp of shock masked my exhale of relief. Not me. For once, it wasn't me, but Marika's ashen expression made my stomach roil with guilt.

I was an awful person. "You don't have to do this, Marika."

Even though we all knew it needed to be done, there was no way I was forcing this onto someone. Who knew what this Death would do to us?

She licked her lips and rolled up her sleeve. "Do it. Do it before I chicken out."

Rivers stepped forward with his dagger, and using the book as a guide, cut the symbol into her arm. Marika winced but didn't make a sound. Her attention was fixed on the circle, on the figure inside who now only had eyes for his anchor.

Rivers stepped back. "What now?"

Oleander flipped the page. "Blood from the wound. Marika, you need to smear it onto the circle. Break the circle with it."

This was the moment for her to chicken out. It still wasn't too late, and the conflict was clear in her beautiful face. But Death, impossibly beautiful Death, took a step toward her, his face morphing from amused to compassionate. He nodded and held out his hand reassuringly. A whimper fell from Marika's lips and then she stepped forward, swiped blood off her arm, and rubbed it across the glowing lines of the circle. A crack like lightning, a rumble like thunder, and the circle went dark.

"Where'd he go?" Ryker asked.

Marika let out a squeak, because there he was, standing right beside her. But he looked different. Slender, dressed in jeans and a long-sleeved roll-neck shirt. His hair was silver now with a definite metallic sheen to it. It was long at the top, swept back off his forehead, with a short back and sides. His eyes were piercing, icy blue, reminding me of the Husky dogs I'd seen in books. Was this what Marika saw? Had he taken on the physical representation of what his anchor perceived, or was it his real form?

"There is much death here." The first words out of his mouth were like a melody. "Much death to feed my hunger."

"Aren't *you* death?" Rivers asked.

Death smirked. "A human name gifted to me over the millennia. I will permit you to use it. But death is a human condition that occurs whether I am present or not. I am merely a collector of souls."

We had him here, and we needed to get down to business. "That's good because we have a ton of lost souls in our city that are in dire need of a thorough collecting. They don't belong here, and they're feeding off human energy and causing problems."

"And where is *here*?" He turned in a slow circle, taking in the bars and ropes and pillars that made up the training room. "This is a lost place. A hidden place. A place which has slipped into a crack of reality."

Yeah, he wasn't referring to the room. "We'll happily fill you in on *where* we are once we have your agreement that you'll take the souls away."

"Take them away?" His smile was pure predator. "Well, of course. I will claim what is mine. And there is much of me here. This place is saturated with the potential of death …" He licked his lips.

What was he talking about? "When can you get started?"

He turned to Marika. "As soon as my anchor permits." He inclined his head. "Should I get started, anchor?"

She took a step away from him. "Yeah, you can … go do whatever."

He laughed, the rise, fall, and cadence making me want to melt. I shuddered.

Death leaned in to Marika. "Let me explain how this works. As my anchor, you come with me, *wherever* I go."

Shit.

Marika shot me a panicked look.

I took several steps toward them, but Death held up a hand to halt my progress, his expression suddenly hostile and as dark as an abyss.

The playful persona was a facade, and a monster lurked beneath. My primal instincts warned me to back up, to run, but I held my ground. We had summoned him. *We* controlled him … didn't we? "Can't you do this without taking her with you?"

His pale eyes were flinty. "No."

Fuck. If we wanted the lost souls gone, then we'd have to trust that he wouldn't hurt Marika. Hurting her would surely break his connection to our world, so it wasn't in his favor. Besides, Oleander had the spell to force him to leave if he refused to go willingly, which both Abbadon and Lucifer had said he would. But Marika looked as if she was about to pass out; all color had drained from her face.

"Marika?" Oleander prodded. "You don't have to do this. We can stop this now."

She swallowed hard. "No. I'm good. I can do this."

Death gave her a half-smile and then locked gazes with me. "Tick-tock." He held out his hand to Marika, dismissing me. "Are you ready to reap?"

"No." But she took his hand and they were gone.

Tick-tock. Death had been speaking to me. He'd been looking at me. My hands were suddenly cold and clammy. This was about the power inside me. I knew it, but how the heck did he know about that? We needed to learn more about this entity before he returned.

I grabbed Lucifer's arm. "What did you see when you looked at him? When he was in the circle."

His jaw tensed. "It's not important."

"Maybe you don't think it is, but humor me anyway. Tell me."

He sighed heavily. "Light. I saw pure, glorious, blinding light."

Was that it? "Then why did you look so shocked?"

His throat bobbed. "Because there is only one other time that I have seen a light like that, and that was in the presence of our creator."

"What? What are you saying?"

He shook his head. "Nothing. I'm saying nothing. It was simply an observation."

An observation that had shaken him. It was evident in the tightness around his eyes and mouth, and the tick in his jaw.

"And what if it's more than nothing? Don't you want to know for sure?"

Abigor walked up to us. "No. We do not. We broke a vow by being here today, and that is as far as it will go."

"Whatever Death is, he is not our concern," Lucifer said. "Once he has rounded up the souls, we will send him back from where he came."

I released Lucifer's arm. "You mean *we* will send him back, because you guys can't actually *do* anything right now." It was a low blow and guilt followed hot on the heels of my words. I pinched the bridge of my nose. "I'm sorry. I shouldn't have said that. It's not your fault you can't play a more active role. It's just … Bane would have wanted to know. He would have needed to understand and connect the dots because he'd understand that it may be important, that everything connects somehow. That what's happening here isn't just a coincidence; we've been drawn here together for a greater purpose. Jonathon, Bane's psychic friend, knew it. He knew it, and he was killed because of it."

It was as if shutters had closed behind his eyes. "I'm not Bane, and you'd do well to remember that."

The anger was back, and fuck the guilt. "Oh, I remember, and you know what, it's a damn shame, because right now, we could really use him."

My skin was suddenly impossibly tight as if

blood was swelling in my veins and pushing outwards. Dark spots appeared in my vision. Wait, this wasn't anger, this was something else. It was...

Tick-tock.

"Harker!" Lucifer made a grab for me.

Had I been about to fall?

"Serenity, what's wrong?" Orin asked. His hand was a comforting presence on the small of my back, but bees were buzzing in my ears, making it impossible to think.

Help us, my daimon's voice implored. It had been days since she'd spoken. The power. The divine power was blocking her, taking up all the space inside.

"What the fuck?" Ryker exclaimed. "Her hands. Look at her hands."

But I couldn't see, because the world was dark and I was floating.

Tick-tock.

"What's wrong with her? Dammit, Lilith. Fix this." Lucifer's dulcet tones were gruffer than usual, edged with fear.

I wanted to open my eyes …Wait. Were they already open?

"The power inside her is too vast," Lilith said. "She can't contain it."

"So, what's going to happen?" Ryker asked.

"No. No, no." Ambrosius's voice was close, right by my ear. "He couldn't have known it would end like this. Did he know? Did he intend you as a sacrifice? I can't believe he would be so cruel."

"What the fuck are you talking about, Ambrosius?" Rivers snapped. "Explain yourself."

"Merlin created a new weapon when he sent the power into the aether," Ambrosius said. "He created Serenity, but he must have known that a mortal body, however powerful, would not be able to contain God's grace."

"The power is made of God's grace?" Orin's tone was stunned. Had I never told him that?

"Yes," Lucifer said. "The White Wings claimed it was a residue left behind when our creator left. They claim they used this residue of His grace to forge the weapons they gave to Arthur, but that is a lie. They stole the grace from God's right hand, Adamah. Every mortal was fashioned in Adamah's image, male and female. Adamah was the prototype, but God had other plans for him, and He kept him close. When the creator vanished, so did Adamah, and I believe they stole his grace, the grace gifted to him by our creator."

"Adamah? As in Adam and Eve?" Cassie asked.

"There was never an Eve. Although Adamah *was* promised a mate, the creator left before fulfilling that promise."

"And what was this Adamah supposed to do?" Orin asked.

"I have no idea, but I suspect the Powers know. I suspect they must still have him hidden away somewhere."

"What has any of this got to do with Harker?" Cassie asked.

Thank you, please get back to me. Why can't I see? Why do I feel trapped?

Cool hands cupped my face. "She's dying," Lilith said softly. "I can feel it."

"Her body was not built to contain such vast amounts of power," Lucifer said.

"No. She is a cambion," Ambrosius said. "Recycling power is what her body was made to do. Merlin knew this, because he too was a cambion. It's why he chose a cambion to become the weapon."

Lilith gasped. "Of course. It makes sense now. The problem is that she isn't recycling the power fast enough. When a cambion feeds, their body can either store that power in its pure form or convert it to energy to fuel their supernatural signature."

"So, you're saying she's not active enough?" Orin said. "That's bullshit. She's out there every day. She barely stops to sleep."

"And she hasn't fed for weeks," Rivers added, his tone reflective.

"It's not enough," Lilith said. "The power is regenerating faster than she can recycle it into energy for herself. Faster than she can use it up to kill shades. She hasn't needed to feed because what she is managing to recycle is feeding her already, fueling her already."

"What can we do?" Lucifer asked.

"I don't know. But for now, we can help her by forcing her to expel some of it."

"Expel it where?" Lucifer pointed out. "That power is lethal. It kills White Wings, shades, and Black Wings."

"But not nephs …" Orin said softly. "It may not kill nephs."

No. Orin. He couldn't. I wouldn't let him. But the pressure of his large hand was on my abdomen.

"What are you doing?" Cassie's voice was shrill. "Dammit, Orin. She could kill you."

"And if we don't try this, then she could die."

"Wait." Another hand was laid on my thigh. "Maybe more than one outlet will limit the damage?"

Ryker … Ryker's hand was on my thigh.

"I'm in." Rivers's hand wrapped around my

arm.

This was crazy. This would hurt them, and that would hurt me. I'd rather die than risk their lives.

"Serenity, can you hear me." Orin's breath tickled my ear. "Let it out, babe. Just let it out, please."

No. I couldn't. A low moan drifted up from my lips, spreading out into the darkness that seemed to pulse and stretch. Pain lanced through my limbs, and my heart pumped so fast it was ready to burst.

"She's going to blow if she doesn't vent." Cassie sounded genuinely concerned now.

"Dammit, Harker. Expel the power. Do it now!" It was Bane's voice. His issuing-orders tone, and my body reacted on instinct by tensing in challenge. "Harker, please ..." Still Bane. Was he back? Had he come back for me? "Harker, survival at all costs, dammit."

I couldn't hold it any longer, it was pushing at my limits, stretching me at the seams, and if I didn't expel it, then I would explode into a tiny billion pieces. Self-preservation, nudged by Bane's voice, reared its head.

Please, my daimon pleaded, tipping me over the edge.

I let go.

The power rushed out of me, channeling itself into the guys from the three points of contact on my body. My relief was accompanied by grunts and growls. It was hurting them. I was hurting them. The world swam out of the darkness, and my vision snapped back into focus to see Ryker's gritted teeth, the top of Orin's head, and Rivers's pale face.

Enough. I shut off the connection and they fell back, their moans echoing in my ears.

"Shit," Ryker muttered.

I sat up, woozy, but no longer fit to explode. Orin pulled me into his lap and smoothed back my sweat-dampened hair. My clothes were stuck to my skin with perspiration. Gross.

"You're okay." Lilith appeared before me, crouching down in her skin-tight slacks. "You're okay for now."

"You can't do that again," Cassie said. "Look at them. They look fried."

I could feel her accusing gaze on the top of my head, and my close friend, Mr. Guilt, came out to play.

"It's okay. You had no choice," Orin said. "We had no choice. We're not losing you."

Rivers rubbed the top of his head. "I need to run."

"Me too," Ryker said.

"You'll use it up," Lilith said. "In a few hours, you'll be back to normal, but Cassie is right. If we do this again, we risk the power causing internal damage. You aren't cambions, and your bodies aren't made to recycle this kind of power on a regular basis."

We needed a long-term solution. "What do we do?" My voice cracked.

Lilith's mouth twisted. "I don't know."

"Then we'll do what we need to until we have a solution," Rivers said.

The other guys nodded in agreement, but there was no way I was doing this again. No way was I putting them in danger a second time. Merlin had created a weapon to stop the shades. He hadn't cared about what happened to that weapon once the threat was averted. That hadn't been his priority. I was dispensable. Always had been. A pit opened up inside me, dark and bottomless and numb. It was the same feeling that had been at the edges of my consciousness in Sunset when I thought about the family that I'd lost, the family that may have abandoned me to Arcadia. Drayton had been right. Nothing was a coincidence. Not my being here, not the power inside me. It all had a purpose, and that purpose was going to kill me.

I pulled myself to my feet. "There won't be a next time."

"Serenity?" Orin made a grab for my hand.

I evaded him, softening the rejection with a smile that felt like rubber. "I'm sorry. I just need to be alone for a while."

I was going to die, because the power inside me was already growing again, like a particularly resilient fungus. I was going to die, but my body was too overwhelmed to feel anything more. The fear would come, and when it did, I'd rather be cloistered in my room, away from sympathetic eyes.

Leaving them all behind, I headed to the safety of my chambers.

"Serenity?" Ambrosius's voice was tentative. "How are you feeling?"

I switched to aether-sight and looked up at him, standing by the foot of my bed, an apparition of blue-hued energy. "Like a dead woman walking. No, that's a lie. I feel nothing. I feel numb."

"I'm sorry. I didn't know. I should have checked on you. I should have realized something was wrong. Why didn't you say something?"

"I was going to, but then stuff kept coming up, important stuff that needed dealing with, and then … Well, it wouldn't have changed the inevitable outcome anyway. I was doomed from the moment I was born."

"Serenity … I don't know what to say."

"You don't have to say anything. I've been sitting here waiting for the terror to hit. I just want to get it out of my system, you know, cry or scream or whatever, but it's like my emotions aren't my own right now. It's like everything is on lockdown." I swung my legs off the bed. "I guess I'm just gonna have to do what I was created to do. Kill the shades and go out with a fucking bang."

There was a knock on the door.

"Come in."

Ryker stepped into the room and closed the door behind him.

"I don't want to talk about it."

"Then don't. Just listen." He walked over to the bed and crouched by it, taking my hands in his. "We are going to find a way around this, Serenity. Oleander and the Order are working on it as we speak, and we will find a solution. Until then, you owe it to us to stay alive, and we will do whatever it takes to keep you with us."

I tried to pull my hands free. "No. I won't risk hurting you."

He held fast. "That's not your choice to make."

The anger that his words promoted was a relief; it was better than feeling nothing. "It is my damn choice. This is *my* burden, *not* yours."

He pinched my chin between his thumb and the crook of his index finger. "No. It's *our* burden. We're in this together." He swallowed hard. "We love you, and we will not lose you."

My eyes pricked—fucking traitorous emotions, switching back on now. "Not fair. You can't pull the L card now. Don't tell me, you were saving it for a moment just like this."

His eyes crinkled. "I'm glad I did, because you need to hear it now more than ever. I love you, Serenity, and I'm sick of losing the people I love. I will *not* lose you. It's three against one. You're outvoted."

We don't want to die, my daimon whispered. Damn her. Damn her for saying the words trapped in my throat. Damn her for forcing me to acknowledge that fact.

I stroked his face. "I don't want to hurt you."

"You'll hurt us more if you die." He ran his thumb across my chin. "Please, please don't die. I need my snuggle buddy."

My laugh was partly a sob. "Just find me some shades to kill. If I keep on top of this, we can buy some time."

He kissed my forehead. "That's more like it." He hauled me up. "And we may have just the solution."

I arched a questioning brow.

He pulled a piece of paper from his pocket.

"This just arrived." He handed it to me. "I'm not sure how he got past the wards. The Order is checking them as we speak, and it's probably a trap but …"

I unfolded the paper and read the neat script.

Abbadon held where we imprisoned Arachne. He must be saved or all is lost.

"It's Drayton's handwriting," Ryker said softly.

My pulse was racing. "Drayton, not Xavier, wrote this. Only he would know what we did with Arachne."

"Orin filled us in on what happened outside the cemetery. But for all we know, shades have access to all their host's memories. We can't jump to any conclusions. This could easily be a trap."

"Or it may be Drayton reaching out to us." God, I wanted it so bad to be him. "What did Lucifer say?"

"Didn't show it to him. He's not the one in charge. You are."

The fucking reins burned a brand in my hands. "We go. We have to be sure. But we play it safe, and we take backup, just in case."

He gave a brisk nod. "The others are waiting in the lounge. Let's plan this right and bring home another win."

The beach was eerily silent, with only the *swish* and *whoosh* of the water and the gentle *whoo* of the wind to ruffle the stillness. Ryker, Orin, and Rivers trekked back and forth across the sand, the exact spot where the sinkhole had taken us into the tunnels where we'd met Arachne months ago. She was still there, trapped in the prison we'd created for her, dreaming in her self-imposed sleep.

"There's nothing here," Rivers said. "The sinkhole is gone. That entrance has gone."

"There has to be some other way in," Ryker mused.

"We've checked out all the other entrances. They're all gone," Orin pointed out.

"Then we find a new way in." I strode toward The Deep. "If there was no way in, then Drayton wouldn't have sent us the note."

"Xavier. Xavier sent the note," Rivers pointed out.

I stopped and glared at him. "It was Drayton's handwriting. He was reaching out to us. I know it.

Why else would he have mentioned Arachne?"

"Because Xavier has access to Drayton's memories, that's why, just like the thing inside Cassie had access to hers."

It was more than that. Orin and I'd both heard him, we'd seen him, but Orin was silent now, doubt sitting like a shadow on his face. Rivers and Ryker exchanged a look, one that said, *just humor her, she's hurting*. And yeah, I was, about so many things, but I was right about this.

Wasting time on arguing with them was pointless. "Think what you want, but *I* know that Drayton penned that note. He's fighting Xavier's hold on him, and we have to get to him. We have to get him out."

"There is no way to remove a shade without killing the host soul," Ryker pointed out. "You know this."

I pinched the bridge of my nose. "No way that we know of. But we can bring him back, lock him up if we have to while we figure it out."

"Serenity," Orin said tentatively. "We're here to save Abbadon. The note *specifically* said we had to save Abbadon."

I was done arguing about this. It was time to pull the leader card. I straightened and pushed back my shoulders. "We'll save Abbadon, but we're taking Drayton too." My tone brooked no argument.

I'd grieved Drayton when I believed he was lost, but if there was a chance to bring him back, however small, then I'd take it.

"I know this is hard," Ryker said. "We all miss Bane. Fuck, if there was something we could do to get him back again, then trust me, we would."

What? Momentarily thrown, my hard-woman persona slipped. "This isn't about Bane."

"Isn't it?" Orin said.

I threw up my hands. "Forget it. Let's just ask some questions and find a fucking way underground." I continued down the dunes toward The Deep.

"We could try hunting The Breed," Ryker suggested. "If we catch one, we can make them show us a way underground."

"No point. They've already gone to ground, either with the shades, or hiding from them. No. We find out how to get into the tunnels and then we call in for backup."

Protectorate units were on standby, with Cassie in charge of deployment, and so were the Black Wings. This involved getting Abbadon back—one of their own. Once we had a way into the tunnels, they could aid in the extraction, but if there were any humans down there in need of saving, it would be on us. If only we hadn't blown out the elevator at the Order. The damn thing had led straight down into the Order lair, which connected to the network of underground tunnels. At the time, we'd been running for our lives, and disabling the elevator had been the only way to stop our pursuers. No point whining over what was done. There had to be another entrance.

The neon-green glow swept across me as I climbed the steps up to the building. No patrons hanging out outside. No music. What the heck? If not for the lights, I'd have thought Jonah had closed up. The guys followed me into the building, into a bar filled with people sipping drinks and talking in hushed tones. The door swung shut behind us, and all conversation stopped as everyone turned to look at us. Nephs, the place was filled with nephs, but something was off.

"What can I do for you guys?" Jonah said from behind the bar. He smiled, but it didn't reach his eyes.

My scalp prickled, my gut clenched, and I instinctually slipped into aether-sight. My soft gasp had the guys flanking me, but it was too late, the patrons were on their feet, moving so fast it was hard to keep track. We were penned in, cut off from the exit. Prisoners.

Jonah placed his palms flat on the bar and leaned forward. "We knew you'd wander down here eventually. Asher will be pleased," the shade inside him said. It was large, like the one that had been inside Drayton.

"What are you? One of his generals?"

He grinned, showcasing a maw of inky black teeth. "No. But I see a promotion in my future. Your future, however, is beginning to look bleak."

I cocked my head. "I think you're forgetting who the hunter is here." I held up my hands and wriggled my fingers. "By all means, let's tangle."

Instead of slipping, his smile widened. "Oh, we haven't forgotten. We're willing to sacrifice a few to get what we want."

"And what is that?"

Clinks and clanks and the scrape of metal on leather filled the room as the nephs withdrew blades of all shapes and sizes.

"Your hands. We want your hands."

Like hell they were getting any part of me, and

the guys were thinking the same, because axes and swords came out to play and the games began. Forty—no, fifty—against four. Odds sucked. But there was no diving out of the deep end, it was sink or swim, and my blades echoed the sentiment as they sliced and cut and gutted. The wounded fell back, but it wouldn't be long before they attacked again. These weren't grunts like the one Rivers had interrogated. These healed fast.

A blade scraped my wrist, drawing blood. The fucker was going for the end game. Like heck I'd let him have my mitts. A shoulder charge had him pinned to the nearest table at an odd angle, enough time to get my hand on his face and do a search. Empty. The neph soul was gone, so it was a burn-the-shit-out-of-the-shade scenario. His scream was a bloody symphony, and the power surged and swelled, wanting out, wanting more. These weren't the same level as Xavier. I'd be able to expel them if the neph was still inside. Bane had said not to take the risk, every minute counted, but these were nephs I'd failed. I could have found them and severed their shadows, but I'd focused on the team, the Lupin, and the Protectorate. I'd left the rest to fend for themselves. This was my fault, and if I could save their lives, then I'd do it.

To the left, my daimon warned. But I was already swinging, driving my blade into an eye. I fumbled, grabbing his wrist and searching for a soul. Empty. The seconds spent delving cost me. He kicked out, catching my knee, sending a sharp pain up my leg and forcing me to buckle. I recovered in time to slam my fist into his gut with a blast of power that sent the shade packing into oblivion.

"Cut them up, cut them down!" Ryker was shouting.

He had the idea. Wound them badly enough and I'd have enough time to root and exterminate. Damn, it felt good, too good. This was me, this was my purpose, and it filled me with a euphoric joy. Movement at the bar. Jonah was retreating.

Like hell.

Using a fallen shade as a spring, I vaulted onto a table and used the other tables as stepping stones until I hit the bar, sprang off it, and landed on a retreating Jonah's back. He didn't go down. The fucker was strong. Instead, he swiped at me, grabbing a fistful of my hair and yanking me over his head. My back slammed onto the ground, and the air vacated my lungs in a rush. The world faded to black.

No. My daimon channeled her power into my limbs, forcing me to roll, to evade the wicked curve of the scimitar aimed for my throat. It hit the linoleum with a dull *thunk* in the exact spot where I'd just lain. I was up in time for him to charge me, but he never made contact. Orin snagged him around the throat and pulled him back.

"Now, Serenity. Do it now," Orin urged.

I slapped my hand to Jonah's chest and looked into his eyes, but not to kill, to search. Was Jonah inside? The others seemed to be gone, but he was strong. Was he trapped like Drayton was? This shade wasn't a general, not yet. He was a nobody like the rest of them, which meant I could expel him, if need be. And there it was, the flicker of light that indicated Jonah's soul was still present.

His eyes widened. "No. Please, kill me. Just kill me."

"Sorry, no can do." Switching to aether-sight, I grabbed his shade essence and yanked him out of Jonah's body.

His roar of rage echoed in my ear, and Jonah sagged in Orin's arms. Around me, the clash of battle had calmed. I surveyed the fallen, unconscious, badly wounded shades whose host bodies were in need of time to heal. Ryker and Rivers stood in the center of the carnage, blood-spattered, chests heaving, biceps bulging. Rivers locked gazes with me, his pale eyes stark against his crimson-smeared face, and grinned. A shiver rushed up my spine, because, in that moment, it wasn't Rivers staring at me, it was the Mind Reaper. But then he blinked, and Rivers was back. He inclined his head in a we-did-it gesture.

But it was far from over. I had my work cut out for me. Expel or burn.

"Stay with Jonah. See what he remembers. I need to deal with the rest of the shades."

Orin nodded and helped Jonah to the nearest upright chair.

I rolled up my sleeves. It was time to earn my keep.

Twenty minutes later, the room was filled with recovering nephs and several dead bodies. A low-grade headache was tickling my temples from spending so much time in aether-sight, but it was worth it to have saved so many lives. The daggers did their work, and shadows were sliced and all was good with the world. Yeah, if only it were that easy.

Jonah sat nursing a bottle of whiskey. He was pale, and his hand trembled every time he raised the bottle to his lips.

"They took her. They took my wife, and others … There were others here, they took them too. Humans and neph. The rest is strange and blurry."

Orin patted the huge guy on the shoulder. "Do you know where they took them?"

Jonah frowned and looked up. "They took them down … down into the basement." He was on his feet in a flash. "The basement! She could still be there."

He made a beeline for the door around the side of the bar, his boots thumping against the ground. After a stunned second, we followed.

We found him standing in the center of a neatly arranged space. Barrels were piled on one side, boxes of nonperishable bar snacks on the other.

"Not here ... She's not ... Where could they have gone?!" He turned in a circle. "They came down here."

Orin strode into the room and began to search it, running his hands across the brick walls and peering behind the barrels. If they'd come down here, there had to be an exit somewhere.

"Over here!" Ryker called from the back of the room. A huge unit with tools and crap was pushed against the wall, and beyond that was the unmistakable outline of a door.

"Jonah, where does that door lead?"

He blinked at the door. "I ... I've never seen it before. Where did it come from?"

Bingo. "Orin, Ryker, can you move the unit please."

The guys did their thing with the muscles and the straining, and on any other day, it would have been a popcorn moment, but too much was riding on this being our answer, and my nerves were stretched too thin.

The unit came away with a scrape and a whine.

Orin tried the door. "It won't budge. It's locked."

"Let me." I flicked my daggers into existence and sliced out the door handle.

Ryker hooked his hand into the gap and pulled. This time, it came away easy, letting in a draft of musty air and showcasing nothing but darkness beyond.

"My wife, she's in there. Isn't she?" Jonah said.

I placed a hand on his forearm. "We're going to find out soon, Jonah. We just need to call for backup and then we can—"

But he was already gone, pushing past Ryker and through the door before I could stop him. The darkness swallowed him as if it were a living entity, and a scream locked in my throat.

"What the fuck just happened?" Ryker said. "Jonah! Hey, mate, can you hear me?"

This was it. This was the entrance Drayton had been talking about. Some kind of arcane magic had created it, and Jonah was gone, transported to wherever this thing sent its minions.

"Rivers, make the call. We need to get in there now."

Rivers wandered off to the other side of the basement, phone pressed to his ear. His Protectorate gear-encased body melded into the pockets of shadows cast by the barrels.

Boot falls echoed down the stairs and several neph entered the basement.

"Hey, guys. Please, go back upstairs."

"Like hell," one of them said. "These fuckers took over our bodies and paraded us around like puppets. I could feel it eating away at me, and there's still so much missing." He rubbed his temples. "You took our shadows so they can't get in again, right?"

"Yeah, you're safe from infection now."

"Good, because we're coming with you, and we're gonna kick some shade arse."

Oh, shit. "I appreciate that, but this could be a trap. We need to do it by the book with MPD personnel."

Doubt flitted across his face but it was gone pretty quick, replaced by determination. "Fine, but we're not going anywhere. We're staying put, and if any more of those fuckers come sniffing around The Deep, then we're taking them out."

Should I point out there was no way for them to identify an infected, not for sure? Should I point out that even if they did, they had no way to kill one? No. They needed something to do, some action they could take to make up for what had been done to them. Maybe to make up for what they'd done while infected? And now that I looked into their eyes properly, taking the time to really see them, the pain, the sorrow, the guilt—it was all there, swirling around like a bottomless whirlpool.

"That's all very well but—"

"It would be great." I cut Ryker off, and shot him a small smile to soften my interruption. "This place means something. The Deep has always been a sanctuary, and the shades tainted that. So yeah, you guys need to watch over it. Make sure it stays a safe zone while Jonah isn't here to do it for you."

They nodded, puffing up their chests and grunting in satisfaction.

"The Protectorate will be here any moment. If you could show them down …"

They retreated with purposeful steps. Crisis averted.

"Good call," Orin said. "They need something else to focus on. They need to feel like they're making a difference."

I had no idea what it felt like to have a shade

inside me, taking over my mind and body, taking over what I was, but it was an invasion of the sanctity of an individual's mind. It would be a while until they felt cleansed.

Rivers joined us. "Cassie and her unit are already on route. They didn't hear from us and got worried. So, they headed out. She thought we'd end up here. She's bringing some Order members with her, as well as Oleander and Ambrosius. They've figured out a tracking spell, which will be extremely useful considering we have no idea where we'll end up when we go through."

I nodded. Tracking was good. "We'll send a small unit in, and then the units left behind can track exactly where this thing takes us."

"What about getting back out?" Ryker posed the question on all our minds.

"We'll figure out an extraction plan when we know how the tracker works."

It was a long shot, and we all knew that despite what measures we took, once we stepped through that door, we'd be on our own. At the mercy of the shades. If it was a trap. If I'd been wrong about Xavier being under Drayton's control. Then we were all fucked. He must have known about The Deep, and yet he didn't warn us. Had this been the trap? Had he hoped we'd never make it past the bar? It didn't matter, we had a way into Asher's sanctuary, and if there was even a slim chance that Abbadon was down there, that Drayton was down there, then we had to take it.

A commotion at the top of the stairs pulled me out of my reverie, and then Cassie's voice drifted down to us.

The backup was here, and we were about to find out what lay beyond the darkness.

My arm still stung from the symbol Rivers had etched into it. It was a tracking rune that the Order had found and infused with power using their connection to arcane magic, but Rivers had given it an extra boost with his rune mojo. Let's hope it worked once we stepped through the doorway. Orin, Ryker, and Rivers were going in with me. Lucifer and four Black Wings I knew by sight alone would be coming too, their focus on getting Abbadon out once we found him. The rest was up to my team.

Oleander spread the parchment with the symbol inked onto it onto the floor. Our blood had been smeared on it, and below it was a map of Midnight.

"Are you sure this is going to work?" Cassie asked for the hundredth time.

It was Ambrosius who answered, his voice coming from the doorway. "I'm certain. The rune is powerful and charged with their blood. The map has been marked with the rune, and spelled. Once you enter the doorway, your location will appear on the map. We have the MED on standby with diggers just in case we can't find a way down to you."

It was the best plan we were going to get. "Hopefully we'll be able to come back this way."

Lucifer and his Black Wings stepped up to the door. "Are you ready?"

I touched his arm to get his attention. "How

about my team leads the way? After all, we have more of an idea of where we left Arachne."

Lucifer opened his mouth to argue but then snapped it closed. Instead, he inclined his head and moved away from the door. "After you."

Taking a deep breath, I stepped into darkness.

It was like stepping into treacle. The darkness clawed at me, pushing at my eyelids and trying to slip up my nose and down my throat. Gagging and coughing, I fell to the dusty ground. Out. I was out.

The guys hit the earth beside me.

"Shit, that was gross." Orin swiped at his chest and arms as if trying to brush off the darkness.

A shudder ran over my body. "We're good. We made it." But *where* were we? Ryker offered me a hand, pulling me up, and we surveyed our surroundings, lit by wall sconces. Someone had gone to the trouble of illuminating this area, which meant it was significant. A wide tunnel with three possible exits. This was familiar. We'd been here before, but then we'd traversed most of this area. Still, three exits rang a distinct alarm bell.

"We should split up," Lucifer said from behind me.

"Yeah, great idea," Ryker drawled. "Let's split up in the tunnels and get picked off one by one." His tone was dripping with sarcasm.

It was the first time Ryker and Lucifer had actually spoken directly to each other, and Ryker, cool, levelheaded Ryker, was positively simmering. A new kind of alarm went off in my head now. Had Ryker been avoiding Lucifer too? He'd said he had no problem with the guy, but the expression on his face now, and that disgusted tone, said different. His reaction to Lucifer's suggestion was totally over the top, because it wasn't really about the suggestion, it was about the person who'd made it.

"Why so hostile?" Lucifer asked. "If you have an issue with me, then I'd prefer it if you'd spit it out."

No, no. Why would he say that? I took a step forward, intent on insinuating myself between the guys, but Rivers pulled me back, his grip firm. It gave Ryker the break he needed to get in Lucifer's face. Big and blond up against tall, dark, and winged.

Ryker lifted his chin, because yeah, Lucifer was that teensy bit taller. "Yes. I have an issue with you. You were supposed to be useful. The whole fucking reason for bringing you back was so you'd get the White Wings on board, but you failed."

The Black Wings who'd come with Lucifer moved forward to flank him.

But Ryker didn't seem to notice, and if he did, he didn't give a shit. "You can't do anything to help the humans. In fact, you can't do anything at all. All you do is give speeches to your Black Wings and hang around the mansion looking broody. There *is* no point to your existence. It's Bane that we need. Bane who was out there every night putting his life on the line. That's who we need. And if you can't be that guy, then you're no good to us."

Lucifer's eyes blazed, the violet irises standing out in the gloom of the tunnel. His jaw tensed and his lips thinned, and for a moment he looked so much like Bane that my heart began to race, but then he pulled it back. His expression smoothed out into the cultured mask that was typical Lucifer, and the light in his eyes dimmed, leaving the bitter taste of disappointment on my tongue.

"Bane was always a temporary measure," Lucifer said, his tone clipped. "I'm sorry for your loss, but you need to get over it. We need to work together the best that we can. Like it or not, I am the leader of the Black Wings, and although I may be redundant when it comes to direct intervention between the humans and the threats of Midnight, my skills will be invaluable when the shades attack the winged."

"And until then you can sit back and twiddle your thumbs," Ryker sneered.

This wasn't the diplomatic neph I'd come to know. This was a man who missed his friend.

"I'm here, aren't I?" Lucifer countered.

"Yeah, to grab your Black Wing and leave."

The pulse in Lucifer's jaw began to tick. "Do you think we enjoy sitting on the sidelines? We fought a war for centuries, standing side by side with the neph against the White Wing threat. We are no cowards. We agreed to stand down to give humanity a chance to be truly free because we trusted in the tenacity of mankind, and I refuse to apologize for that."

I'd had enough of this. "I think splitting up is a

great idea. Lucifer, you take the left tunnel. We'll take the middle. Give it ten and then head back this way to report back."

Ryker's stiff shoulders relaxed a little, and he stepped away from Lucifer, exhaling heavily. He rubbed his eyes with thumb and index finger. I watched as the fight bled out of his Adonis features. "I'm sorry. Now isn't the time to get argumentative."

And he was back. Thank goodness, because we needed him on form. This really wasn't who he was. Ryker wasn't the kind of guy to get easily riled up, but I'd been so caught up in my feelings I'd neglected to see how Bane's loss was affecting the others. Selfish, selfish me. It was something to rectify once we made it out of here.

Slipping my hand into Ryker's, I tugged him toward the center tunnel. "Ten minutes. See you back here." I cast the words over my shoulder to Lucifer.

We dove into the cool interior of the central tunnel and switched on the flashlights, because there were no wall sconces here. Either the shades could see in absolute darkness, or these tunnels weren't used by them, but by something else that didn't need light to see. Another shudder, this time up the back of my neck. Thank God we'd cleared this place of spiderlings. Thank goodness Arachne was gone.

"I'm having flashbacks of the last time we were here," Orin said.

"I feel like we've taken this route before," Ryker added.

And then the reason why became evident as the tunnel walls became decorated in beautiful patterns.

Arachne's silk.

This was the way to her chamber, the one we'd walled her into. My feet faltered.

Rivers cursed. So, he'd realized where we were too. Why were my feet faltering? Drayton had instructed us to come here in his note. To the place where we'd trapped Arachne. This was the place, so why was my gut telling me to turn and run?

And then it was too late, because we were in the chamber, surrounded by piles of rubble. Rubble that had once been the wall that had held Arachne captive. My heart crawled into my throat and beat a staccato rhythm. An all too familiar scuttling filled the chamber, and my hackles rose. No. It couldn't be. We'd dispatched them all.

But there they were, Arachne's children, crawling down the walls to meet us, leading the way for the main act, the spiderling mother herself. She dropped from the ceiling and landed with a wet plop in the center of the room. Her body was swollen beyond measure, lit up from within, where her babies could be seen writhing and eager to be born, and the rest … The rest clung to the walls and hung from silken threads.

It was a nightmare. A throwback to that awful time beneath the ground when she'd almost ended us all.

"This cannot be happening," Orin said through gritted teeth.

But it was.

"Second chances do not come along every day," Arachne hissed. "And yet here you are, just as my love promised me."

"Your love?"

"My king. My liege. My Asher. He found me like he promised he would. He has liberated me as he promised he would, and our children will liberate us all."

Their children? As in him and her with the procreation? Urgh! We backed up, weapons at the ready. There would be no defense against her toxin if she chose to spray it, but she seemed perfectly content watching us squirm.

The word *trap* came to mind and my heart sank, but now wasn't the time to curse my misplaced convictions.

It was time to keep her talking, so we could formulate a plan to get the fuck out of here. "Asher doesn't care about you or your spiderlings. All he wants to do is end the winged. Everything else is background noise. Everyone else is dispensable."

"Not me. Never me. I'm essential. He came for me, and he cares enough to make my spiderlings his. He cares enough to infuse them with powerful essence. They are now part of his army."

What was she talking about?

"Serenity," Ryker said from my left. "I have a bad feeling about this. Switch to aether-sight or whatever you do."

I slipped into the aether, and my heart stopped for a long beat, and then slammed into my ribs, hard. Oh, shit. Oh, fucking shit. Her spiderlings were hosts. The spiderlings were fucking shades!

"Serenity?" Orin prompted.

Asher's silence in response to us moving the humans to Respite made sense now. The humans had been a filler for him, weak alternatives to what he could truly have, and while we'd been scrambling above ground to take away his advantage, he'd been burrowing beneath it to get to his true prize. He'd called Arachne to Midnight. She'd been his plan all along. Arachne was the mother of his army. And she was carrying a second batch. How the heck was I going to incinerate these? How could I get my hands on them without getting my face chewed off?

"Shades, they're all shades."

"It was a fucking trap," Rivers snapped.

And we were surrounded.

"Asher will be pleased," Arachne said. "Your dead bodies will be my gift to him."

The spiderlings attacked, but not as a mass like they'd done the last time. This time, they attacked with precision and formation. They attacked with a plan. They attacked like an army. There was little time to formulate, only time to react. My daggers cut into limbs and sliced hides, but where one spider-shade fell, another took its place. There would be no reprieve for us, not from this horde.

"Make for the exit!" Orin bellowed. "Just cut through to the exit."

It was the smart plan, but it meant leaving Arachne alive, it meant leaving the vessel that could swell Asher's army intact.

I couldn't do that.

Arachne had to die, and I knew just how to do it.

She was cursed, invincible, or so she thought, but viewing her in the aether, the cracks in her armor were evident, and her soul, her humanoid soul, was bound in this horrific shell. My hands itched. I could free her.

Just needed to get close.

Just needed to get my hands on her.

"Cover me!" I didn't wait to see if they heard, there was no time. If this was going to work, then the action had to happen now while Arachne thought she had the upper hand. While her guard was down.

Rolling to avoid the stab of a spiderling's talon-tipped leg, I skidded across the dusty ground and smashed into Arachne's bulging abdomen. Her body tensed, and she spun, ready to spear me with her fangs, but my hand was already inside her, passing through her armor and into the place where her true essence resided. She froze, her heartbeat echoing in my head, and then I made the cut, the daggers slicing through the thread that bound her to this body—a body that had never been hers. Her sigh filled my mind, and then her legs curled in on themselves as she dropped.

Shit. I threw myself back just in time and slammed into a wall of muscle. Screams echoed off the walls and the spider-shades attacked with vigor.

"Grunts. These are grunts," Rivers yelled. "They take longer to heal. Hit them hard, and we can make it out."

The bloodshed began in earnest as we cut our way toward the exit. Ryker and Orin were swallowed by the mass. Damn, please let them have made it out. More spider-shades dropped from the ceiling. Rivers let out a bellow as he was swept away from me, and then I was alone—an island in a sea of killer crawlers. But there was no way I'd be going down without a fight. My body went into auto mode, the pain of every scratch or stab muted by adrenaline. No toxin. They weren't spraying, which was a small mercy. It gave us a chance. It gave the others a chance. Please let them have made it out. A spiderling knocked me flying, and as my body arched through the air, I saw my guys by the exit, fighting, pushing, desperate to get back into the room. Desperate to get to me.

"Go!" My voice a boom. "Get out. Now!" I surrendered my life to fate, hitting the ground in a crouch that jarred my knees. Fate would decide if I'd live or die; all I could do was fight. The seconds blurred, time stopped, and my limbs grew sluggish, slower. My thighs quivered. Pain lanced across my back, bringing tears to my eyes and darkness to my vision. My leg gave way, and I stumbled to the ground.

Surrounded. I was surrounded, and yet, they

hesitated. Why? I looked up into the nearest spiderling's eyes, slipping into aether-sight to see the shade's face twisted in wonder. It scuttled forward, and the others moved back. Was this their leader?

I pulled myself up. "What are you waiting for?"

It cocked its head, unable to speak with the body forced upon it … forced. This pairing had been forced. The knowledge hit me sudden and sure. It waited. Trapped in the body Asher had made him inhabit, this grunt, this shade unable to speak out.

It was waiting for death.

A wave of sorrow crested my heart, and I slapped my hand onto its leg, expelling power hot and potent. There was no scream, no protest. The shade burned silently away until he was gone. Silence, deep and complete, followed, and then a roar ripped through the room and the spiderlings scattered. I spun to see Drayton barreling through the gap. Nephs I didn't know fought alongside him, pushing back the threat. He'd come to help. I'd been right, this wasn't a trap.

Orin appeared by my side. "Time to get the heck out of here."

My feet left the ground as I was slung over his shoulder, and we sprang into motion. We made it to the tunnel, to Ryker and Rivers, but we just kept going.

"Stop. Wait. We have to wait for Drayton!" I hammered on Orin's shoulders.

"No. We need to get out of here before Asher gets wind of what's happening and sends reinforcements."

We came out into the sconce lit-chamber, and

Orin set me on my feet.

"We can't leave Drayton."

"That isn't your friend," Lucifer said from behind me.

I turned on him to find him carrying a figure over his shoulder. "Drayton is in control. I know it. Why else would he have just helped us?"

"Because not all the shades agree with what Asher is doing. Xavier is one of them. He helped us get to Abbadon, but there's no time to explain it all now. It's imperative we get Abbadon out of here."

The stubborn mule inside me kicked and stomped. "It is Drayton. He's *making* Xavier feel this way. We can't leave him to Asher's mercy. He helped us, we need to help him."

Ryker sighed. "She's right. We can't in good conscience just leave."

"Yes, we can," Rivers countered.

"Orin?" I looked to the gentle giant for support.

His expression clouded. "We need to get you to safety, and we need to get the humans out."

Humans? I noticed them for the first time now, hovering at Lucifer's back with Jonah and his wife.

I met Lucifer's gaze. "You saved them?"

Lucifer shrugged. "I didn't do anything. I liberated the neph, Jonah, and he opened the cages to set the humans free and then they followed me out here."

Humans were our priority, there was no arguing with that, but they didn't need me to get them out.

I summoned my daggers. "Get the humans to safety. I'll be right behind you." It was my leader tone, and no one questioned me this time. I took a step and the world rumbled.

"I think that's our cue to leave," Rivers said. "Diggers."

Cassie had the MED digging to get us out. Dust and rock began to fall from the ceiling.

"Get back!" Ryker cried.

I jumped out of the way in time to avoid a chunk of rock the size of my head. It hit the ground and rolled, and then the whole fucking ceiling began to cave. Who the heck had decided to use diggers? Bad idea, this had been a fucking awful idea. Coughing and gagging, we backed up as far as we could. We were about to be buried alive. Another rumble, this time farther away, was followed by shrill screams.

"The other chamber is caving in," Rivers said. "It'll buy us time."

Us, but what about Drayton and the shades that had helped us? My pulse a jackrabbit, I pushed past Ryker and ran toward the tunnel. I was less than a meter away when the whole thing caved in on itself, rock and rubble and choking dust. My scream lodged in my throat and died.

"Harker, move it now!" Bane's voice jarred me into action.

There was no getting through that. No getting to Drayton. That knowledge was like losing him all over again, a crushing sensation that clamped around my lungs and squeezed. I spun on my heel and headed back. Voices echoed down toward us from the hole in the ceiling, and then a rope ladder appeared.

Lucifer passed Abbadon to one of his Black Wings, who began to climb, and then he propelled me up the ladder.

We'd got what we'd come for, but I'd lost Drayton all over again. I'd failed him again.

"I'm sorry," Lucifer called to my back. "I truly am."

The fire in the hearth crackled, echoing my dissent with pops and crackles as it devoured the kindling. The guys had stationed themselves about the room, their gazes wary, not used to seeing me so agitated, but Lucifer was the calm totem in the storm. He watched me coolly, levelly, and it was driving me nuts. I needed a blowout, a raging argument, the kind I'd have had with Bane.

"We left them to die." I paced the lounge, anger and guilt a hot ball in my chest.

"They're shades," Rivers said.

"And you were the Mind Reaper. People change. They helped us. They want to stop Asher."

"I understand they could have been valuable," Lucifer said. "But we had a mission, and we had to stick to it."

Valuable? "I don't care about how *valuable* they'd be. I care that they put their lives on the line to save us and we ran. We left them to die."

"They're shades. I doubt they can die," Rivers pointed out.

"So we left them trapped for eternity. Yeah, that makes it all better." I threw up my hands. "What is wrong with you people?"

Ryker and Orin exchanged glances, and Rivers

just crossed his arms, unfazed. It was Lucifer who answered.

"In every war, there are casualties. Xavier helped us to set Abbadon free, he helped us escape at the cost of his life because he knew it was the only way to prevent Asher succeeding. He sacrificed himself so Abbadon could be free and you could live. Your ability is paramount, and Abbadon was important to Asher's experiments."

"What experiments?"

Lucifer's jaw ticked. "To find a way to infect the winged."

Infect the … If he did that then he could simply take over. Just slip in and have it all. Ice filled my veins. "How far did he get?"

"Too far, but not far enough we hope."

"You hope?"

Lucifer pinched the bridge of his nose. "We can only wait and see what happens from here on. He has data, blood samples, but winged blood doesn't last long outside our body. It evaporates, and so he'd have to work fast with what he has in his lab."

"He has a lab?"

"Yes, the tunnel we took led to it. It was where he was holding the humans. Jonah was already there with Xavier when we arrived. Xavier was actually the shade charged with Abbadon's care. With Jonah's arrival, he knew we were on our way. He met us there with some of the rebel shades, and the rest you know."

I ran a hand over my face. "We dealt a blow, then?"

Lucifer nodded, a small smile playing on his

perfect lips. "You killed Arachne, and we found Abbadon. We took away their advantage."

"Stalemate," Rivers said.

Relief flooded me, my knees gave way, and I plonked my butt on the sofa. "I need a drink."

The door slid open, and Cassie stood there. Her face was pale and stunned.

"Cassie?" Orin took a step toward her, but she shook her head and moved aside to reveal the reason for her shock.

A figure stepped into the room. Disheveled, bloody, but alive.

Drink forgotten I slowly rose off my seat. "Drayton?"

His lips twitched in an attempted smile, and then his eyes rolled and he dropped like a stone.

No one moved for a long beat and then the guys rushed forward as one and hauled Drayton onto the largest sofa.

I wrung my hands. "He made it. He actually made it."

Drayton's face was covered in grime, his hair was coated in dust, but even in this state he was beautiful. His chest rose and fell evenly, alive, here. He'd found his way back to us.

A hand fell on my shoulder. "That's Xavier, Serenity. Not Drayton," Orin said softly. "We need to be wary; we can't let our guard down completely, not yet."

I exhaled and nodded. "Yeah. I know." I cupped Drayton's cheek and leaned in and pressed a kiss to his forehead before stepping back. "Lock him up. We'll speak to him when he regains consciousness."

Orin and Rivers scooped Drayton up off the sofa just as Marika came striding into the room, eyes flashing.

"How the heck did he get through the wards?" she demanded. "I knew it! The wards must be weakening."

"Not the wards." Death strode in behind her, his silver hair glinting in the firelight. "Your wards are tight." He leaned back against the wall by the doors as Orin and Rivers disappeared through the exit with their load.

Marika shot Death an irritated look. "Yeah, well, excuse me if I don't take your word for it."

I blinked at her, surprised by her tone. When she'd left with Death, she'd been barely able to utter two words to him without swallowing in fear, and now she was berating him?

Death caught my eye and shrugged. "I guess spending a few days in my company has loosened your friend's tongue."

"Days?"

Marika sighed. "Three, to be exact. No, four, I think." She shook her head. "I can't explain it, but we kinda had to go backward and forward through time, but not on this plane, on one sitting alongside it." She cracked her neck. "We got them all, though."

"We?" Death arched a brow.

She rolled her eyes. "Really? You want to go there?"

He ran his tongue across his teeth, and she snapped her mouth shut. There was a story here, an adventure, and once we eliminated the shade threat,

I'd sit down and make her tell me. But right now we had an unconscious shade to deal with.

"You got all the souls," Lucifer confirmed.

Death's eyes narrowed. "Yes."

"In that case, we can relieve you of your duties."

"I'll go find Oleander," Cassie said.

"No!" Marika cried.

What the heck? "No? What do you mean, no? We have to send him back."

She caught her bottom lip between her teeth. "You can't. If you do ...then you'll be sending me with him."

Marika plonked herself onto the wingback. "It's my fault. I should have checked the texts with greater care. Oleander found the ritual, and we combed through it, but we missed the clause about the anchor being a sacrifice to Death. If you send him back, then you send me with him."

Death arched a brow and smiled. "She *is* riveting company, and it's been a while since I had any female *companionship*."

I couldn't help but suspect that his lascivious tone was a put-on. It was at odds with his expression, his body language, his whole damn demeanor. But what choice did we have? There was no way we were sending Marika wherever he had come from.

Marika buried her head in her hands. "I'm sorry."

I crouched in front of her. "Don't be. You did great. You all did. Because of Oleander, you, and the Order, we managed to summon Death, and he claimed the souls. It's another win for us."

Now the humans would be able to fight back

when Asher turned his attention to them, because he would. We'd taken away his spider army-making machine. Most of the nephs were shadow-free now, and the ones that weren't, would soon be. He had only one focus now, and we'd make damn sure he had to work for it.

"What about the souls?" Ryker asked. "If we keep Death here, then how does he take the souls with him?"

Marika raised a brow at Death, who shrugged and lifted his shirt to reveal a heavily inked, muscled torso. No. Not inked. This wasn't ink, because it moved and writhed. Lines slipped over lines that formed incomprehensible symbols.

"What the fuck?" Cassie said softly.

"The souls are mine, and those that were not have been dispatched."

The souls were *in* his body? "How? Why?"

His eyes lit up with ice fire. "Because they belong to me. They *are* me. My essence. My grace."

"Who are you?" Lucifer asked in a hushed tone.

Death dropped his shirt, a wry smile playing on his lips. "A guest, it seems, at least until you tire of your friend and decide you're willing to send her with me after all."

Panic flared in Marika's eyes. "Serenity …"

I grasped her hands. "You are not going anywhere." I shot Death a stern stare. "And if you're going to be staying for a while, then you'll need to make yourself useful."

He inclined his head. "I sense there is much death to come. Out there, and in here." His eyes bored into me. "And when it does, I will be here to claim it."

A chill encased my body, shivering over my skin. Me … He was referring to my ultimate demise. He was referring to the power that would kill me. I lifted my chin. "You'll be surprised how hard Midnighters are to kill."

"I don't doubt it, Miss Harker. I don't doubt it."

Abbadon was recovering, Xavier was unconscious and healing, and we were alive. A small victory to be celebrated, one I'd encouraged. The training room was filled with music and laughter. A premature celebration maybe, but life was too short to wait on the big win. We needed to stop and celebrate the little successes too. We'd put a huge dent in Asher's plans tonight and we'd come out alive. Marika was still going over the sanctity of the wards, refusing to take Death's word that they were strong, trying to figure out how the hell Xavier, a shade, had managed to get through, but I knew … I knew how. Drayton was growing stronger, and the shade was weakening. The wards had sensed Drayton, and they'd let him in. Simple. I just needed to make the others see it too, and once Xavier woke up, I'd prove to them that Drayton was in the driver's seat.

Washed and dressed for bed, I stared at my naked face in the bathroom mirror. The power was growing inside me again, replenishing. It was only a matter of time before it killed me. I had maybe a week at the most before I'd need to expel it or feel the pain. If I ignored that, if we didn't find a shade to kill, then it would be me that it burned through. Oleander and Ambrosius remained locked in the cliff house library looking for answers, and their tenacity gave me hope that maybe, just maybe, I'd live to see a sunrise.

Blowing out an exhausted breath, I pulled open the door to head into my bedroom and stopped short. Orin, Ryker, and Rivers had made themselves at home on my bed. Orin stopped dealing cards to grab a handful of popcorn from the bowl perched on the bedside table. Rivers munched crisps from another bowl.

Ryker patted the bed next to him. "You coming?"

My heart soared and filled with love for these men who knew just when I needed them the most.

"Yeah, I'm coming."

I awoke to soft snores and warm embraces. Rivers and Ryker were on either side of me and Orin's head was pressed to my abdomen, his body farther down the bed. My fingers were tangled in his silken hair, but it was easy to slide them free. He moaned softly, but then fell back into slumber.

They were shattered, and if not for the excess of power in my limbs, I'd be out like a light too. But I needed something. I needed to see the moon. I climbed over Ryker, brushing a kiss across his forehead, grabbed my gown and slippers, and headed for the roost.

The corridors were thick with silence and heavy

with sleep. Was I the only soul awake? The steps to the roost flew by beneath my feet, and I pushed open the door to the tower, eager for the air and the stars. My body tensed, suddenly on alert. Someone was already here.

Tall, large, and winged. My breath caught painfully, and then I bit the insides of my cheeks in chastisement.

"Lucifer, what are you doing up here?"

"I couldn't sleep." He sighed. "That's a lie. I could, but every time I do I dream."

Shame colored my cheeks. I'd been hard on him. We all had. He'd done what he'd had to in order to ensure humanity had a shot at survival. He'd sacrificed a century of consciousness. It wasn't his fault that Bane had been so fucking awesome, that he was so desperately missed.

I walked up to the balcony and leaned against it to look up at his profile. "You want to talk about it?"

He tucked in his chin. "Yes. But you're probably not the best person to do that with."

My curiosity was officially piqued. "And why is that?"

"Because my dreams … they're about you. About us." He made a sound of exasperation. "About you and Bane."

My mouth was suddenly dry. "That must be difficult for you."

He turned his head to look at me, his brows snapping down. "You're worried about my feelings? After all that you've lost?"

I shrugged. "You lost stuff too. You lost a century of memories. You lost a century of living."

He smiled wryly. "To be honest, it was pleasant being able to rest and hand the reins over for a while. Immortality can become tedious."

"When I'm feeling antsy, coming up here to look at the moon always helps."

Lucifer lifted his chin to gaze up at the proud round disc. "It looks much better if you get closer," he said softly. He looked down on me, a series of indecipherable emotions flitting across his handsome face. "I could take you closer ... If you like?"

My stomach flipped hard, and the pulse in my throat began to thud. This was a Bane-and-me thing. Our nightly ritual when we couldn't sleep. But Lucifer looked so hopeful and so anxious at the same time that to turn him down ... I just couldn't.

"Sure, that would be great."

He grinned, flashing fang, and my heart skipped a beat. Fangs ... He had fangs ... But his arms were already around me, his scent filling my head, and the roost was far below as the moon reached out to us.

To be continued...

**Join Serenity in the thrilling conclusion to her adventures in *Savior of Midnight*.
Scroll down to check out the first chapter.**

The delicious aroma of cinnamon greeted me as I took the steps down into the kitchen. Oleander must be making breakfast ... No, wait. It couldn't be him because he was at the cliff house, and it wasn't Orin because I'd just left him in the shower.

Heart pounding in my chest like a drum, I stepped into the room to find Lucifer at the stove flipping golden discs and catching them expertly in Bane's favorite skillet. He was making pancakes? But it wasn't just the pancakes that had my breath catching; it was the floral apron that he'd tied around his waist—Bane's apron.

He turned at my approach, as if sensing my presence and our gazes locked. For a moment he looked lost, confused, and then he smiled and there they were—fangs. Bane's fucking fangs. Did he know he had them? Did he realize?

He placed a plate of pancakes on the table. "Are you hungry?"

I remained by the door, hand on the frame.

"Have you always made pancakes?"

He frowned. "Harker, do you want pancakes or not?"

Stupid question, of course I wanted pancakes. But he hadn't answered mine. "Lucifer?"

He flinched and averted his gaze. "I wanted to cook this morning. I wanted to make pancakes ... for you." The last part was a growl.

Bane used to make me pancakes. "You have fangs ..."

He reached up to touch his mouth and then ran his tongue down the elongated canines. The pulse at my throat jumped with a pang of desire, and his attention zeroed in on my neck.

Silence, absolute in its intensity, fell over us. It stretched like taffy, growing thicker by the second until it begged to be broken. "What's happening to you?"

He tucked in his chin, his shoulders rising and falling. "I don't know." He tore off the apron, threw it onto the counter and brushed past me. "Enjoy the pancakes."

Rivers entered a moment later. "I smell pancakes."

I gestured toward the plate piled high with deliciousness. "Lucifer made them."

His brows flicked up. "I guess that's something he and Bane have in common."

I slowly shook my head and swallowed hard. "I think it's more than that. He also has fangs now."

Rivers's brows snapped down and his mouth parted slightly in comprehension. "You don't think that he's—"

"Don't." I held up my hand. "Don't say it. I'm can't allow myself to even contemplate it. I don't want to get my hopes up."

Rivers nodded sagely. "Fine, we'll stick a pin in it for now. We have plenty to keep us busy in the meantime." He eyed the pancakes almost wistfully. "We've let Xavier sweat for a day. I think it's time we began our interrogation."

Did I really believe Xavier was a threat? No. But there was no way we'd let him parade around the mansion without making one hundred percent certain that we weren't letting a mole into our den. For that we'd need information he may not give us if we just accepted his arrival at face value.

I nodded. "Being locked up for a day and night should have softened him up enough to talk."

"He's a general," Rivers said. "If he doesn't want to talk, then he won't. We may have to resort to force." His eyes flashed with lethal intent.

Hell no. "Even if he hadn't come to us willingly, that's Drayton's body you're talking about torturing. So, no."

Rivers exhaled through his nose.

I held up my hands. "Look, I don't think he's a threat, but I need to know why he really chose to help us, and why he came here of all places."

Rivers's eyes narrowed. "You think Drayton's pulling the strings, don't you?"

I blew out a breath. "I don't know, but I intend to find out." I sat down and picked up a fork. "Stop eyeing them up and grab a plate. We'll eat first. Interrogation on an empty stomach is a bitch."

Xavier looked at me through Drayton's eyes, and disconcertion was a live thing writhing in my stomach.

"Why am I locked up?" he asked softly.

I crouched outside his cell. "We just need to know a few things before we can let you out. Like why you came here?"

He frowned. "There *is* nowhere else for me to go now."

He sounded sincere, like he actually believed what he was saying, but I'd been burned by pretty-faced liars before. There had to be another reason he'd come to us. "Bullshit. There are plenty of hidey holes for you to squat in. Places where Asher won't find you. Why come here?"

He closed his eyes briefly. "Because you have wards. Because it's safe here."

My pulse jumped, reminding me of the reason for the others' disconcertion when it came to him being here. Our wards hadn't been tripped by him. He'd simply walked in undetected. I had my suspicion as to how. Yeah, totally Drayton related, but I needed him to confirm it. I needed him to admit something, the one thing that was a certainty in the depths of my mind.

I gave him my best incredulous look. "Safe? For you? Really? You're a shade and you come to the one place that the only weapon that can kill you resides?" I shook my head. "Bullshit."

He sat forward, eyes flashing. "You won't kill me, Serenity, not just because killing me would kill

Dayton, but because you owe me and you're sense of honor won't let you hurt me."

"Wow, you really think you have me pegged, don't you?"

He made a sound of exasperation. "I helped you, and because of that my cover has been blown. Asher knows about the resistance now. He knows where my loyalties really lie. He will weed out the shades who side with me, and he will kill them if we don't get them out. So, yes, I came here because it's time for you to return the favor."

"We? There is no *we*. Not until you level with me."

"I am levelling with you."

Rivers coughed. I glanced up at him to see the telltale gleam in his eye, and for a split second, it was as if the Mind Reaper was looking back at me. A shiver skittered down my spine, and Rivers frowned. Crazy, I was being crazy. It was Rivers, just Rivers. I tore my gaze away, fixing it back onto Xavier. My intuition was rarely wrong, there was more he wasn't telling me, but Xavier's attention was on Rivers now, and his face drained of color.

I snapped my fingers to get his attention. "Hey, Xavier, eyes on me."

He blinked and focused. "Look. I'm not the enemy. Not all shades are the same. We don't all want the same thing."

Okay, now we were getting somewhere. "And what do you want, Xavier?"

He seemed to consider the question, cocking his head slightly as if choosing his words. "When I first arrived in Midnight, I wanted vengeance. I wanted to make the winged pay for usurping our place. I wanted our creator to feel the pain of loss when we tore his new pets to shreds. Humans would die, Asher had warned. He explained how sacrifices were necessary for the good of the many. And I believed him. I believed that the end would justify the means. But the longer I spent here, in this body, the more I experienced this world and the more my doubt grew. I wasn't the only shade to feel it. The massacre of humans and shades no longer feels like vengeance. It feels like a waste. And Asher's goals have shifted. Power has gone to his head. Whereas before he was content to wipe out the winged and fall back into our role as protectors of humanity, now he feels that humanity is too corrupt to be saved. He wants to wipe them out too, and I just can't allow that."

"Why? Why do you care so much about humanity?"

Irritation flashed across his beautiful features. "Have you not been listening? Because humans were *our* charges. *We* were their guardians once."

Understanding the shades could be the key to bringing them down. Maybe there would be some nugget, some Achilles heel that we could use. "Tell us. Help us to understand."

He sighed and leaned his head back against the wall. His eyes fluttered closed. "It feels like a lifetime ago, and at the same time it could have been yesterday when we were born. He made us from shadow. From the darkness that cocooned his light. We were his first children, the very first, and he loved us. I know he did. We were his eyes and ears, his guardians, his assassins. We watched over each cycle of creation, and there were many. Some monstrous beyond description, some so beautiful they made me ache with longing in a way that made no sense to me."

"Other creations?" Ryker joined me on the ground. "Like animals?"

Xavier chuckled. "Some could be likened to animals because they had no higher intelligence, but others were more than just sentient, they had the potential of great power. But our creator wasn't satisfied. Time and time again, he purged the world of his creations, and we, his shades, would sweep over the world and drag the creatures to whatever prison he had created for them. Because, you see, he couldn't bring himself to completely destroy his work. And so he kept his rejects locked up." He tucked in his chin. "And he created man. We watched as this wondrous creature was brought to life with atoms of starlight and a breath of stolen grace, and he was so pleased with this new toy that he permitted us, his shades, to live amongst them, to walk in their wake. Over time, we became bonded to them. We became connected in a way that was almost intimate."

"Shadows ... you became their shadows," Ryker said, his tone hushed in wonder.

Was this why the only way they could access their host was via shadows?

Xavier nodded in Ryker's direction. "Yes. It was a symbiotic relationship where we protected the host, and the host allowed us to finally experience the wondrous world: taste, true sight and smell. It was then that we realized how much *he* had held back from us—the colors ... all the colors that our eyes could not see, and all the flavors that our tongues could not taste. We made the fatal error of asking why? Of asking to be reborn. Of asking to be human."

"He cast you out," Ryker said. "Locked you away."

"Worse than that. He replaced us. He created the winged and it was these new creations that tore us away from our humans and exiled us into an eternal prison. Betrayed." He closed his eyes for a moment, as if the memory brought him pain. "We were betrayed. Our centuries' of service was rewarded with a forever exile."

But if that was true, then how come the winged hadn't said anything? I glanced across at Ryker's thoughtful expression.

"The winged didn't seem to have any idea that you existed," Ryker echoed my thoughts.

Xavier snorted. "I'm not surprised. *He* would have wiped any memory of our existence from their minds, just as he wiped us from human memory. I do wonder why he allowed them to keep their shadows—these imprints we'd left behind, these residues of our existence. It makes me wonder if it was his love for us that made him sentimental."

Sentimental? Was he serious? Ryker, once again, on the same frequency as me asked the question hovering on my lips.

"It seems a bit harsh. Why get rid of you just because you asked to be human?" Ryker asked. "He could have just said no."

Xavier's smile was wry. "Yes. I suppose he could have, but, in the end, we were evidence of yet another failure—the creation that was dissatisfied with its existence. Our request probably reminded him that we were proof of all his previous failures. Locking us away, wiping memories, allowed him to start afresh with a clean slate."

"Arrogance and pride are obviously not just a human trait," Rivers said dryly.

He was referring to God, but his statement could easily be applied to the winged too. They strutted about believing they were the first of God's creation, believing they'd been humanities only guardians. Pride and arrogance. It was impossible not to feel sympathy for the shades, but it was a short burst of empathy, because the past, no matter how unfair it had been to them, didn't excuse what they were doing to Midnight in the present.

"I remember now," Xavier said. "I remember what we were and what we stood for and there are others who are like me. We wish to protect humanity, to live, not inside them, but alongside them. Live like we once did. Asher only wants power. He wants to rule, and I won't lie, there are shades who feel the same. There are many that agree with him, but the majority are either unaware of his real agenda, too afraid to act, or in league with the resistance." He leaned forward. "You have to help me to liberate them. They don't deserve to be used as cannon fodder in a fight no one will win."

The spider-shade who could have killed me came to mind. He'd stopped and waited for me to end him. He'd wanted to be free. And now Xavier was telling me there were others like him, many others being forced into hosts against their will.

He stared at me, his gaze penetrating. "You do

realize you cannot win."

I held up my hands and wiggled my fingers. "I can damn try. Right now we have the upper hand. Arachne is dead along with her spiderlings. Nephs have been stripped of their shadows, and the ghosts that were weakening the humans are gone. The shades' host supply just got cut off."

"Not if Asher succeeds in finding a way to take winged hosts," Xavier pointed out. "We liberated Abbadon from Asher's clutches, but the samples that were collected are still in Asher's possession."

"They'll degrade too fast for him to do anything," Rivers said. "It's a long shot."

"But still a shot," Xavier reiterated.

He was right. The winged needed to be warned and we needed to make more of a dent in Asher's army, force him to think twice before making any kind of move.

I turned to Ryker. "We have to help them."

"No." Rivers said. "You have to kill them."

He was referring to the power building up inside me, the fact that if I didn't expel it, then it would kill me, but Xavier didn't know that, and the horrified look on his face prodded the ready guilt in my chest.

Xavier gripped the bars. "No. You don't need to do that. You don't need to kill anymore shades. We can find a way to free the resistance; many of them have not even taken hosts yet. That will reduce Asher's numbers and throw him off balance, and then we can end all of this by ending Asher. Once he's dead, the threat will be over."

That would be a great plan except ... "I can't

kill him. I tried."

Xavier sat back, his shoulders sagging. "In the tower ... You tried to kill him then?"

"Yes, what the heck did you think I was doing? Moving in for a hug?"

He looked away, but not before I caught a glimpse of awareness in his warm, brown peepers. What wasn't he telling me? What was he holding back? He'd told us a story—his story—but there was more he didn't trust us with. And who could blame him? He'd tipped us off, helped us get Abbadon away from Asher and when he'd come to us, we'd locked him up. Maybe my suspicion was wrong. In which case, it was time to build a bridge. He needed a vote of confidence, and that would involve sharing a crucial piece of information. Information, that if handed to Asher could be used against me. Telling him would show we trusted him, that *I* trusted him.

I locked eyes with Xavier. "I *need* to kill shades to survive. If I go more than a few days without killing one, I'll die."

His head whipped up. "The power will burn through you."

"Yes."

He shook his head. "If Asher finds out, all he'll need to do is go underground with all the shades. He'll wait you out until you die."

"Yes." My tone was soft. "There is no happy ending for me. Trust me. I don't revel in the kill." The lie was ashes on my tongue because, like it or not, the kill brought relief. "The ultimate goal is the protection of humanity, so if you know how to end Asher, you need to share it with me."

Xavier's expression smoothed out. He'd come to a decision and my body tightened in anticipation. "Asher's host body is cambion and can be overcome from within."

"What do you mean?" Rivers asked.

"A cambion is similar to an incubus. They feed off energy to survive," Xavier said.

"A cambion feeds off a variety of energy," Ryker clarified, "but an incubus requires sexual energy to survive."

Xavier cleared his throat. "I believe that changes when a shade enters the body."

How did he know this? My stomach dropped and then hope surged hot and potent through my veins. He knew because he was experiencing the same. My suspicion hadn't been wrong after all. Ryker tensed beside me, and Rivers stepped out of the shadows to stand by the bars. They'd come to the same conclusion, and the air vibrated with expectation.

Xavier blinked and looked away. "I know because it's happening to me."

Bingo! My mouth was suddenly as dry as a dust bowl. This was what I'd been angling for—confirmation that Drayton was having an influence. That he was here, with us, listening. He'd steered Xavier to us, and it had been Drayton the wards had picked up on, not Xavier, because Drayton's essence was now strong enough to mask the shade.

"He wrote the note, didn't he?" Ryker asked. Thank goodness because my throat was too tight to speak.

Xavier shook his head sharply. "No. But he told

me what to write."

I exhaled in a rush. "Can he hear us? Is he here? Can we speak to him?"

Xavier's expression shuttered. "Not right now, he's ... away."

"You're lying," Rivers's voice was cold. "You're afraid that if you let him out, you may not get back in the driver's seat."

Xavier's jaw flexed. "You need me," he said. "I can help you bring down Asher. The resistance will follow *me*."

"Tell us exactly how to bring down Asher," Ryker demanded.

Xavier's gaze was suddenly steely and calculating, the general had finally come out to play. "If you help me free my men, I'll tell you what you need to know to bring down Asher. I'll tell you exactly how you can overpower him from within."

I pushed up off the ground, jerked my head away from the cell, and walked off, indicating the guys to follow.

We stopped outside the basement doors. "What do you guys think?"

"It's too dangerous," Ryker said. "And he could be lying about knowing how to bring down Asher."

"No," Rivers said. "He was telling the truth about that. But he was lying about Drayton. He could let Drayton speak to us if he wanted to." His expression was icy determination. "Drayton is alive, and once we have what we want from Xavier, we're going to get him back for good."

There was silence as we absorbed this fact. That this was real, that Drayton was here, back with us.

223

My pulse fluttered in my throat, my hands fisted at my sides, the urge to pummel Xavier into giving us what we wanted was a living entity inside me, but hurting him would hurt Drayton, and whether we liked it or not, right now we needed Xavier and the manpower he could bring to the table.

"What now?" Ryker asked.

I exhaled away the tension. "We do the job he wants us to do. We liberate the resistance and get the key to bringing down Asher. Follow my lead." I headed back to the cell and stood, feet shoulder width apart. "We've made our decision."

Xavier pulled himself to his feet. "And?"

"We'll help you get your men, but we want more than information from you in return."

He watched me warily.

"You'll tell us exactly how to weaken Asher, you and your men will join our ranks, and ... you'll let us speak to Drayton."

He sucked in a breath. "Yes to the first two terms but the last ... I can't."

"Yes. You can," Rivers said firmly. "And you will. You owe it to us. After everything you've done, all the havoc you've caused, you owe us."

Xavier hung his head and closed his eyes for several long beats. He cocked his head, as if listening to something, several emotions played across his face and then he opened his eyes and nodded slowly. "You have a deal. Half an hour with Drayton once my men are free."

Had he just had a conversation with Drayton? My pulse was a staccato beat.

"There's more," Ryker said. "We need a couple

of shades we can kill."

Xavier froze, his eyes darting to me. "I can't."

"Ryker ..." I reached for him, shaking my head.

He brushed me off. "Deal or no deal?" he pressed.

I couldn't do this. I couldn't ask Xavier to sacrifice his people to keep me alive. "We'll find another way."

"We will," Rivers said with confidence. "But we need to buy you time." He crossed his arms. "Deal or no deal, Xavier?"

Xavier began to pace.

"Look, you said yourself not all shades are the same," Ryker reminded him. "So help us get hold of some of the bad guys. Think of it as a *necessary sacrifice.*"

He was throwing Xavier's words back at him, and it had the desired effect. Xavier paused in his trek and looked across at us, his jailers. "I can get you what you need. I think I have a way we can both get what we want in one fell swoop." His gaze was calculating once more. He was thinking with his general head again.

"Do we have a deal?" Ryker asked.

Xavier nodded. "We have a deal."

I stuck the keys into the lock and twisted. "Welcome to the MPD."

Other Books by Debbie Cassidy

The Gatekeeper Chronicles
Coauthored with Jasmine Walt
Marked by Sin
Hunted by Sin
Claimed by Sin

The Witch Blood Chronicles
(*Spin-off to the Gatekeeper Chronicles*)
Binding Magick
Defying Magick
Embracing Magick
Unleashing Magick

The Fearless Destiny Series
Beyond Everlight
Into Evernight
Under Twilight

Chronicles of Midnight
Protector of Midnight
Champion of Midnight
Secrets of Midnight
Shades of Midnight
Savior of Midnight

Novellas
Blood Blade
Grotesque

The Shadowlands Series
Coauthored with Richard Amos
Shadow Reaper
Shadow Eater
Shadow Destiny

ABOUT THE AUTHOR

Debbie Cassidy lives in England, Bedfordshire, with her three kids and very supportive husband. Coffee and chocolate biscuits are her writing fuels of choice, and she is still working on getting that perfect tower of solitude built in her back garden. Obsessed with building new worlds and reading about them, she spends her spare time daydreaming and conversing with the characters in her head – in a totally non psychotic way of course. She writes High Fantasy and Urban fantasy. Connect with Debbie via her website debbiecassidyauthor.com or twitter @authordcassidy.

Made in the USA
Monee, IL
11 December 2023

48822071R00135